Just when you think life can't get much better, a crashing wave wipes out your sand castle. Former spies Nick Seven and Felicia Hagens are taking a break from Key Largo to visit a casino owned by Nick's friend, Rock Bianco. An unexpected, nasty encounter with one of Nick's former lovers turns disastrous when she's killed shortly afterward. The police and the girl's wealthy father are convinced that Nick did it, despite the lack of hard evidence. The billionaire industrialist wages an online smear campaign to make Nick look guilty, including sordid details from his past career in the CIA. The stakes become more personal when the fallout impacts Felicia, testing their relationship. Nick fights back, but why is the man determined to hold him responsible for his daughter's murder? Who really killed her, and why is their identity being shielded? Can Nick and Felicia resolve this crisis and reclaim their idyllic life in paradise?

The Big Fall
Copyright © 2020 Tim Smith
ISBN: 978-1-4874-3077-1
Cover art by Martine Jardin

Published by eXtasy Books Inc or
Devine Destinies, an imprint of eXtasy Books Inc

Look for us online at:
www.eXtasybooks.com or www.devinedestinies.com

THE BIG FALL
NICK SEVEN BOOK 7

BY

TIM SMITH

DEDICATION

To Maga, for 10 years of great editing.

CHAPTER ONE

Fort Lauderdale, Florida is part of the oceanfront strip known as the Gold Coast. It has long been the destination for fat-moneyed snowbirds who trek south every winter to escape the doldrums of Cleveland or Passaic. Basically a continuation of Miami Beach, it's situated between Hollywood to the south and Palm Beach to the north. Port Everglades is one of the largest departure sites for cruise ships in the United States, serving three million passengers annually. The city boasts over a hundred marinas and sixty-odd golf courses, with a year-round climate that can best be described as pleasant, bordering on sultry. The perfect place for the *haves* to put distance between themselves and the *have-nots* that Hemingway so cynically described.

Three miles offshore sat a former cruise ship that had been converted into a casino boat called the Gold Flamingo. Water taxis and private craft converged on the boat in a steady flow, laden with gamblers hoping to win back what they'd spent on their vacation. The Monday night crowd was clad in a cross between tourist casual and trendy chic, as dictated by the fashionistas. The casinos were filled with the unmistakable sounds of gamblers in heat — coins being fed into hungry slot machines, dice rattling on the crap tables, followed by cursing when someone's number didn't hit. The high rollers dominated the Caribbean Stud and roulette tables. The more conservative bettors plied their skills at the video poker terminals while visions of jackpots danced in their heads. The tinkling of tokens hitting metal trays blended with the bright colorful lights and live music to create a cacophony of greed.

Nick Seven sat alone at a blackjack table with two stacks of chips and a drink in front of him. A small group of people stood around the table watching the action, eager to see who would come out on top in this high-stakes game. Nick looked intently at the dealer, decked out in the customary uniform of a white shirt, black bow tie and black sequined vest. Nick had opted for the Florida casual look of a white linen jacket over a powder-blue shirt and tan trousers. He and the dealer had been sparring for forty-five minutes, and the house wasn't turning a profit on this game—yet. Nick's gaze shifted to the six of diamonds and the four of hearts on display in front of him. The dealer had a king of hearts face up, and another card face down.

"Call or fold?" the dealer asked.

Nick rhythmically bounced a hundred-dollar chip on the felt-topped table while making a decision. "Call," he said as he tossed the chip into the pot.

The dealer dealt Nick an ace of spades, bringing his total to 21, and gave himself a six of clubs. The crowd hushed as the dealer turned over his hole card, revealing a seven of diamonds. "Looks like you beat me again."

The bystanders chuckled in appreciation. Nick smiled and raked in his winnings.

"Another hand?" the dealer asked.

Nick shook his head. "Daddy always said quit while you're ahead." He tossed the dealer a C-note chip. "Thanks for the ride."

He slid his tall, lean frame off the stool, took his chips to the cashier's cage then put the money in his wallet. *Two grand. Not bad for a hundred-buck investment.*

He walked through the casino toward the slot machines, where Felicia sat transfixed in front of a one-armed bandit. Nick's gaze took in her Barbadian beauty—bronzed skin, long brown hair that came to rest on her upper chest, a petite yet

2

trim physique and the most sensual brown eyes he'd ever peered into. She placed coin after coin into the machine and pulled the lever like she was on autopilot. Nick leaned in close and spoke in a low voice so he wouldn't startle her.

"Any luck?"

Felicia pulled the lever again. "Close, hon," she replied in her West Indies accent, her gaze not leaving the spinning reels that had her mesmerized. "This one's about to spill its guts."

Nick laughed. "Right. I'm going to the bar. You want a drink?"

"I'll be along."

He took a seat and ordered a scotch and soda. He looked over at Felicia again and felt a warm glow inside. *When I got conned into coming back to the CIA for one last case a few years ago, I never dreamed anything good would come out of it, but when Felicia and I saw each other for the first time in five years it was like we'd never parted. I really got lucky when she decided to stay with me in Key Largo instead of going back to Barbados when the job was finished.* He smiled. *Maybe that's why they always called me Lucky Nick.*

He turned back to the bar and took a sip. They had decided to take a break from running Cricket's Bayside, the club Nick owned on the Gulf side of Key Largo. He had always liked to gamble, and a trip to The Gold Flamingo seemed like the right diversion. The boat was owned by a friend, Rockland P. "Rock" Bianco, who had formerly owned Cricket's until Nick won it from him in a high-stakes poker game years earlier. Nick glanced at his tanned reflection in the mirror behind the bar and absently ran his fingers through his thick brown hair. His gaze went to the quartet playing soft rock music on a stage next to the bar. But his relaxation was short-lived, interrupted by a female voice over his shoulder. It was a voice he didn't want to hear.

"Hello, Nick."

Nick slowly turned around and came to eye to eye with

Kristine Overman. He slowly looked her up and down, taking in what he'd once known so intimately: her slightly pouty lips, perfectly coiffed long blonde hair that outlined her face, and her skinny beach-bunny tanned physique currently encased in a glittery cocktail dress that would've set most people back a week's pay. It was cut low enough to show off her firm cleavage. A heavy gold rope chain supported a large gold letter "K" spelled out in diamonds resting on her upper chest. She gave him an intense unsmiling gaze that could've melted the polar icecap.

"Hello, Kristine," he replied with no hint of emotion.

"You're the last person I expected to see here," she paused, "or ever wanted to see again."

Nick smiled politely.

Kristine nodded her head in Felicia's direction. "Is that the slut you dumped me for?"

His gaze narrowed. "Careful, Kristine. Your boarding school education is showing again."

Kristine eyed Felicia. "You really disappoint me, Nick. Did you find this one on a street corner in Little Haiti with a mattress strapped to her back?"

Nick tried to maintain his non-committal look while his pulse pounded. *If you were a man, you'd be missing some of those pearly whites by now.*

"But I suppose when you're hard-up, any tramp needing a green card will do," Kristine said.

He smiled ever so slightly. "At least she's not afraid to swallow."

She drew her hand back. "You son of a bitch!"

She brought her open palm toward Nick's face but he quickly grabbed her wrist, stopping her in mid-bitch slap. The bar patrons seated nearby immediately quieted, watching the drama unfolding before them.

"I don't think daddy would appreciate you making a scene in a crowded place like this," he said in a low, intense tone.

"Might be embarrassing to explain at his next board meeting."

Kristine put her arms at her sides, fuming. "No one treats me like you did and gets away with it. After what I gave up for you, then you tossed me aside like a pair of old shoes."

"Get over it, Kristine," Nick chided. "The only reason you took up with me in the first place was because you were bored with that pencil-necked preppy you were seeing. You came after me like a bitch in heat when you saw me manhandle a drunk in my club and thought I'd add some excitement to your dull country club world."

"All the times I put up with those greasy lowlifes in that place of yours. You owe me something for that."

"It was no day at the beach for me, either, babe," he cracked. "I got tired of starching my upper lip around that freak show you call a family."

"At least my family associates with their own kind. You'd shack up with any cheap whore who'd spread her legs, no matter where they came from."

Nick's temper began to escalate, but he wouldn't give Kristine the satisfaction of seeing it. *What the hell has gotten into her? She never went off on me like this before.* "Anything else?"

She took a step closer and jammed her finger into Nick's chest, still wild-eyed. "Nobody walks out on me, and I'm going to make your life hell for what you did."

Nick chuckled. "What are you going to do—bore me to death with a bunch of idle threats?"

"You just watch your ass, Nick. You'll get yours someday."

"Message received. Now why don't you be a good little girl and go back to your snotty friends and your backgammon game before someone accuses you of slumming?"

Kristine turned on her high heels and rapidly strode through the casino. Nick watched her walk away. *I have to admit — she still has a butt you could bounce a quarter off of. Arrogant twerp.*

Felicia joined him. "Who was that?"

Nick hesitated. "Kristine Overman."

"Isn't that the rich society girl you used to hang with before I came here?"

"One and the same."

"Hmph! Didn't seem so classy to me."

"Let us not be too judgmental. What she lacks in charm she more than makes up for with money."

"Shoulda spent some of it on a better dress. What did she mean, you'll get yours?"

Nick sipped his drink. "As I recall, there's an old adage about hell having no fury like a woman scorned. Besides, if Kristine weren't spoiled, obnoxious and self-centered, she'd have no personality at all."

Felicia laughed then took a seat. She ordered a Rum Runner and took a sip when it arrived.

"Any luck with the slots?" Nick asked.

She scowled. "No. I even had a dream about hittin' the jackpot."

"Never trust your dreams."

"How'd you do at blackjack?"

"It was profitable."

Felicia looked around the gaily decorated room. "Nice place, your friend's boat."

"Yeah. Rock Bianco opened this place after I won Cricket's from him in a poker game. Want to step outside? It's getting a little stuffy in here."

They walked through the casino and emerged onto the deck. Nick leaned against the railing and peered into the dark, clear night illuminated by bright stars and an unobscured half-moon. Waves gently slapped against the hull of the boat. A double-decked water taxi boat docked below, laden with more passengers in search of a good time. It was followed shortly by a smaller craft, reserved for high rollers who didn't want to rub elbows with the common folk.

"Tell me 'bout this girl you had words with," Felicia began.

"Not much to tell. We used to go out until I got tired of the whole upper-crust mentality."

"What you mean?"

"Her family is very old money and I'm not. Being around folks like that requires a certain mindset that I'm not equipped with."

Felicia placed her arm around his waist. "You're as classy as they come. Why'd you really drop her?"

Nick hesitated for a few moments, weighing how much of his past he felt like sharing. "It became painfully obvious that Kristine only went out with me to get a rise out of her father, since I wasn't their kind of people. I'm also not into the Bordeaux and art gallery scene, and I think polo is a boring sport." He paused. "Come to think of it, the sex wasn't all that great, either."

Felicia giggled and rested her head on his arm. "Whatever the reason, I'm glad we ended up together."

He placed his hand on her cheek and peered into her soft, almond-shaped brown eyes. "So am I."

"By the way, you handled yourself really well in there. Better than I would have."

Nick felt embarrassed. "Thank you. I'm just sorry you had to see that."

They stood for a few minutes enjoying the peaceful evening. Felicia covered her mouth as she yawned.

"Want to call it a night?" Nick asked. "We can catch the next water taxi."

"Only if you want to." She ran her fingers along his cheek and flashed a wicked smile. "It's kinda early to turn in, but I could probably think of somethin' to entertain you back at the hotel."

"I'm sure you could."

She kissed him. "I'm gonna visit the little girl's room. Don't leave without me."

Nick watched Felicia walk inside, then faced the water again. He used the solitude to reflect on the turn of events that had brought him to this point in life. After his wife was killed in a terrorist attack meant for him when he was stationed in England, he had kept his graveside promise to avenge her murder. Then he had turned in his code book and cyanide pills, and rejoined the human race. He found the club in Key Largo and never looked back. Seeing Kristine Overman only reminded him of the rudderless direction his life had taken at that time, when settling for no-strings one-nighters was good enough. Felicia had changed all that when they were reunited a short time later. It reminded Nick that he had been attracted to her when she worked on his team in London, and he had missed her more than he wanted to admit.

The stillness was interrupted by the sound of raised voices coming from the observation deck, two stories above. He heard a woman shouting "Are you crazy? Get away from me!" A few moments later he heard a shrill scream that was quickly silenced. Nick looked up in time to see a body hurtling from the top deck. It splashed into the ocean, where it momentarily sank then slowly surfaced, floating face down.

Nick quickly stripped off his jacket, climbed over the rail then dived into the water. He paddled his way to the surface, looked around then swam in the direction of the floating body. The currents worked against him. When he reached the person, he grabbed her hair to pull her face out of the water. He wrapped his arm around her waist and began swimming back to the boat. The salt water stung his eyes and he blinked rapidly to clear them.

When he was within twenty feet of the water taxi ramp, one of the crew members tossed him a life preserver attached to a rope. Nick grabbed it and let them pull him to the boat.

Two men took hold of the body and lifted it on board. Nick hoisted himself up then stood, his chest heaving as he hungrily gulped air.

Felicia ran up to him, carrying his jacket. "I told you not to leave without me."

Nick wiped the stinging, briny water from his eyes with his shirt sleeve then fluffed his hair. He looked at the person he had rescued. Her face had been badly beaten, and large bruises had already begun forming amidst the cuts and abrasions. Her dress was torn, there were deep bruises on her throat, and her hair was matted with strands of seaweed. His brow furrowed in confusion when he finally recognized Kristine Overman.

"Is she . . ." he began.

One of the crew looked up at him. "Dead."

CHAPTER TWO

The Fort Lauderdale police boat arrived within twenty minutes, containing officers, evidence technicians and a medical examiner, among others. Nick sat on a bench at the taxi loading area and stared, dumbfounded and disbelieving, at Kristine Overman's body, covered head to toe with a blanket. *Funny how people become so considerate of your dignity when you're dead and can't complain about it.*

Felicia sat next to him and ran her palm along his shoulder. "You okay?"

"Yeah, great. Nothing like a moonlight swim to break up the evening."

"Hon, this wasn't your fault. Don't beat yourself up over nothin'."

"I'll try and keep that in mind."

Men from the Coroner's office transferred the body to a stretcher then carried it onto the boat. Nick and Felicia were approached by two detectives who took their preliminary statements. When they were finished, the older of the two looked at Nick's driver's license and made notes on his pad.

"Is this your correct address, Mr. Seven?" he asked.

"Yeah, everything's current."

He handed Nick his identification. "Are you staying in town?"

"At the Bahia Mar Resort on Seabreeze Boulevard."

"We may drop by in the morning. I'm sure we'll have some follow-up questions."

Nick gave him a cynical look. "I'll look forward to it."

10

He and Felicia walked toward the lounge. Nick's shoes squished and his clothes smelled of salt water. They were approached by one of the casino floorwalkers.

"Excuse me, Mr. Seven," he began. "Mr. Bianco would like a word with you."

Nick looked at Felicia. "You go on inside. I'll be back in a few minutes."

Nick was escorted to Bianco's stateroom below decks. The man knocked on the door, heard a gruff "Come in!" then opened the door.

Rock Bianco sat in a high-back chair behind an oak desk. He was built like a well-fed bulldog, with a jowly face and thinning black hair that was swept toward the back of his balding pate. Bianco was a professional gambler who had started life dealing blackjack in the backs of pool rooms, then graduated to being a Vegas pit boss. Even though Nick had bested him in a poker game and taken away his livelihood, Bianco harbored no animosity, and they had maintained a friendship. He motioned impatiently at a captain's chair across from his desk. Nick slumped into it.

Rock pushed a crystal decanter of whiskey and a matching tumbler across the desk. Nick poured himself a modest amount and sipped it sparingly.

"Drink up, Nick," Rock said in a raspy voice that was scarred by too many years of hard drinking and smoking cigars. "It'll take the chill off."

"I'm good."

Rock downed his whiskey in one gulp then poured another. "That dame in the drink. You know who she is?"

"Yeah, I know. Do you?"

Rock scoffed. "Her old man owns most of the Gold Coast and has all the politicians in his pocket. You bet your ass I know who she is. How do you know her?"

"We used to go out but I hadn't seen her in a few years."

"You didn't know she'd be here tonight?"

"Hell, no. She's the last person I wanted to see. What's this all about?"

Rock took a cigar from the humidor on his desk, bit off the tip, then spat it out. "Some broad from a rich family croaks on my boat. You got any idea what that does for business?"

"Yeah, you'll have big crowds for the next couple of weeks. People like to visit crime scenes more than amusement parks."

Rock glared at him. "If that's a joke, I ain't laughin'."

He tossed Nick one of the cigars then lit his own. Nick examined it. "Cuban?"

Rock took a few aggressive puffs to get it started. "Best cigars in the world."

Nick set the cigar on the desk. "Also illegal. What did you want to see me about?"

Rock opened a drawer, set a stack of crisp bills on the desk then slid it across. "Five grand. That's a retainer. Find out who iced that dame and I'll give you twenty more."

Nick didn't touch the money. "Forget it, Rock. That's not my bag anymore. The police will solve this one out without my help."

"I don't like cops snoopin' around."

Nick picked up the cigar and slowly twirled it between his fingers. "Yeah, I can imagine why. Besides these Cubans, I'll bet they wouldn't find any tax stamps on the liquor in your storeroom, either. Why are you worried about the police? You told me you weren't mobbed up any longer."

"Doesn't mean I have to like cops."

Nick slipped the cigar into his breast pocket for later, then finished his drink. He stood. "Let me sleep on it and get back to you. Right now, I'm so tired I can't think straight. Can you have one of your boats take me and my girl back to the mainland?"

Rock picked up the phone and barked orders for a private boat to be available immediately. He stood and walked around the desk. "Sorry if I came across a little rough, but I haven't had this kind of trouble since I opened this place. If you can't help me out, don't be a stranger. You and your gal come back any time."

Nick grinned. "So I can clip you for another two grand?"

Rock gave a gruff chuckle. "Pocket change."

Morning arrived with a series of powerful knocks on the door to Nick and Felicia's hotel suite. Nick looked through a bleary eye at the clock. *Who'd be calling on us at this ungodly hour?*

He got out of bed, slipped into his pants then stumbled to the door, which was still being assaulted by an untiring set of knuckles. He opened the door and saw the stony faces of the two detectives he'd made friends with the night before. The senior officer was Brannigan and his younger partner was named Cortez. Nick didn't waste time on protocol and held the door open for them.

Felicia emerged from the bedroom rubbing sleep from her eyes and yawning. She hadn't bothered with the formality of dressing. The two detectives looked at each other with raised eyebrows. Felicia gave them an innocent, blank stare.

"You'll have to forgive my friend, gentlemen," Nick sleepily apologized. "We left home in a hurry and she didn't have time to pack. Hon, would you call room service and order coffee? Oh, and have them send up some doughnuts for these officers."

Nick fell into the nearest easy chair while the detectives took seats on the divan. He took a deep breath and tried to wake up for the grilling he was about to get.

"You're quite the smart-ass, aren't you, Mr. Seven," Brannigan commented.

Nick shrugged. "I get by."

"What were you and your lady friend doing on the Gold Flamingo last night?" Cortez asked.

"What everyone else was doing—drinking and gambling."

"Any luck?"

"I did okay, but that isn't why you're here."

"We have a positive ID on the victim," Brannigan said. "Name's Kristine Overman of Bal Harbour. You know her?"

"Yeah, I knew her," Nick answered.

"Mind telling us about that?"

"There isn't much to tell. We used to go out but I hadn't seen her in a few years."

"Not a pleasant break-up?" Brannigan asked.

Nick eyed him warily. "I've had better. Why are you asking?"

Cortez referred to his notepad. "According to witnesses, you two had a fight at the bar."

"I wouldn't call it a fight," Nick replied. "She made a few nasty remarks, tried to slap me into the next room and I stopped her."

"What kinds of remarks?"

"Just a lot of trash talk, nothing noteworthy."

"Really?" Cortez said as he referenced his notes. "The quote we got was *'You watch your ass. You'll get yours'*."

"Right words, wrong mouth. She said I'd get mine."

"For what?"

Nick chuckled. "I never could figure women out. You don't return one phone call and suddenly you're on the shit list."

"Did you know the girl was dead when the crew pulled her out of the water?" Brannigan asked.

"No. I saw the body do a swan dive from the top deck and dove in to save whoever it was."

"Just being a Good Samaritan," Brannigan said with feigned sincerity. "You didn't know it was Kristine Overman?"

"How could I? It was dark out there."

"Where did you say you were when she went in?" Cortez asked.

"On the landing outside the second-floor casino. Correct me if I'm wrong, but didn't we cover this last night?"

"Just routine," Brannigan said. "Any witnesses that saw you hanging around outside the casino when she was tossed overboard?"

Now I'm getting it. "No. My girlfriend had gone inside a few minutes earlier and I didn't see anyone else. And who said she was thrown over?"

"You did," Cortez answered. "At least, you implied it in your initial statement to us. You said you heard the sounds of a fight followed by a scream, then looked up in time to see the body falling from the top of the ship. That's what you claimed to have seen from where you said you were standing."

"Claimed to have seen from where I said I was standing?" Nick repeated. "Look, fellas, I told you everything last night. I didn't know it was Kristine who'd gone overboard, only that someone had. I was trying to do the right thing."

"Sure," Brannigan said. "Anything else you'd care to tell us?"

"Like what?"

"Like how you know Rock Bianco."

"Bianco's an acquaintance. We did some business together a few years ago."

"What kind of business?"

"He used to own the bar and restaurant I have in Key Largo."

"Just a simple business transaction?"

"Simple enough. I won it from him in a poker game. Why are you asking me about Bianco?"

"We're curious why he wanted to see you before you left the boat last night."

Nick stared at Brannigan for a moment. "How did you know about that?"

"It came up during our canvas. You see, that's what we do when someone's been murdered. We talk to witnesses and gather little bits of information, then follow up on it. Perhaps you're familiar with the concept."

"Bianco heard I was on board and he wanted to say hello."

"Nothing more than that?"

"Nothing more."

"We checked you out, Mr. Seven," Cortez interjected. "You didn't tell us you were once with the CIA."

"You didn't ask."

"CIA," Brannigan echoed. "Kill a lot of people when you were a spy?"

Nick gave him a cool gaze. "Just the ones who deserved it."

"I'll bet they teach you spies a lot of different ways to kill, don't they?"

Nick worked to keep his temper under control. "What're you getting at?"

Brannigan leaned forward and rested his forearms on his knees. "Kristine Overman was strangled by a pair of very strong hands either before or after she did a half-gainer off that boat. If she was being a pain in the ass, this would be an easy out for you."

"Before or after?" Nick quizzed. "You aren't even sure if she was dead before she hit the water?"

"The Coroner's report isn't finalized yet," Cortez replied. "It's possible she was still alive when you went in after her."

Nick glanced down for a moment. "I didn't know that, and I don't make a habit of killing people who annoy me."

"Maybe you were just trying to be thorough," Brannigan commented. "You know – *Always get your man. Bring 'em back dead or alive.* Isn't that what they teach you spies?"

"And don't they teach you cops that I'm entitled to a

lawyer?" Nick shot back.

"That's only if you're under arrest," Cortez replied.

Nick stared hard at him. "Then either arrest me or get the hell outta here."

The two detectives stood.

"Thanks for your time, Mr. Seven" Brannigan said. "How long are you planning on staying in town?"

"Couple of days, but if I decide to leave, I'm sure you'll have no trouble finding me."

Nick let them out just as room service arrived. Nick signed the bill, then took the tray to the balcony. Felicia joined him, having donned a light blue sundress. She accepted the coffee Nick offered her. On the beach three floors below, the early sun worshippers were claiming their spots, marking their territory with beach towels and folding chairs.

"What was that all about?" Felicia asked.

Nick sipped his coffee. "They think I killed Kristine."

Felicia hesitated. "You didn't, did you?"

"Don't be ridiculous," Nick snapped. "I wish I'd never laid eyes on her. If you're my best character witness, I'm in deep shit."

Felicia squeezed his hand. "You know I've got your back, hon. Weren't those the same questions they asked you last night?"

"Uh-huh. They just want to make sure my lies are consistent."

"They gonna keep hasslin' you?"

"Only until they come up with a better suspect."

Captain Donald Kruger sat behind his desk at the Fort Lauderdale police station with his phone glued to his ear, listening to the party on the other end. The wall behind his desk was practically a shrine, boasting several commendations and the Medal for Valor for taking a bullet in the line of duty ten years earlier. Brannigan and Cortez entered the office and Kruger indicated two chairs across from his desk.

"Yes, sir," he patiently said into the phone while running a hand over his bald head. "I understand she was your youngest daughter and I'm very sorry for your loss. We're working some leads but it's too early to come to any conclusions. No, I really don't think a call to the state Attorney General would expedite matters. As soon as I know something, I'll call you personally. No, thank *you*, sir."

He forcefully hung up, then addressed the detectives. "That was J.P. Overman, father of the deceased. He wants to know what we're doing to apprehend the son of a bitch who did away with his pride and joy. What do I tell him the next time he calls?"

"Tell him we're working on it," Brannigan answered.

"Good, Phil. That and twenty years will get you a pension. What did you find at the murder scene?"

Cortez consulted his note pad. "Cigarette butts, a woman's left shoe that likely came off during the struggle, the victim's purse, and a cell phone that had been stomped on."

"Where did you find it?"

"Near where her shoe was found. From the location, it appears she was holding it, dropped it during the struggle and her assailant stepped on it. The lab's working on it."

"What was in her purse?"

"Keys, lipstick, hairbrush, a compact, and a wallet containing credit cards and two-hundred-and-sixty dollars. There were also two small bags of cocaine, total weight, ten grams."

"Anything else?"

"Not yet," Brannigan answered.

"Do you guys remember a little thing called suspects? Do we have any?"

"The former boyfriend, Nick Seven," Cortez replied.

"Right now, he looks pretty good for it."

"How good is pretty good?" Kruger asked.

"He had an argument with her in the bar," Cortez said, "and he can't provide an alibi witness to account for his whereabouts when it went down."

"What kind of argument?"

Cortez referenced his notes. "The witnesses said Overman made some disparaging remarks about Seven's girlfriend, they argued about it, she tried to hit him, he stopped her, and she made a threat to get even with him."

"What else?" Kruger asked.

Brannigan took a deep breath then answered. "According to Seven, he and the Overman girl used to be an item but they had an unpleasant break-up. Maybe he was in the casino, she confronts him, pisses him off, he gets her on the upper deck then kills her."

"Why would he kill her?" Kruger pressed.

"Maybe Overman had some dirt on him and threatened him with it for dumping her," Brannigan replied.

Kruger shook his head. "That's pretty weak. What would she have on this guy that would be worth killing for?"

"Seven's a former CIA spook," Cortez answered. "Phil might have a point. If they were close, no telling what kinds of things she knew about him. Maybe she threatened to go public and expose him for dropping her."

Kruger exhaled an irritated breath. "All I'm hearing from you two is maybe, maybe, maybe. This woman was killed on a gambling boat full of passengers. What the hell have you guys been doing—taking extra coffee breaks?"

"Come on, Cap," Brannigan said. "We were out there half the night, talking to the employees and customers. It's gonna take time to sort through their statements and do follow-up interviews."

"I'll assign two more teams to help. What about the

security cameras?"

"We looked at what was shot of the murder," Cortez said. "All it shows is the girl getting killed by a man. No face shots."

Kruger paused. "Since she had drugs in her purse, check with narcotics, and talk to her father. Maybe he can shine some light on it."

"Who's supplying all the heat?" Brannigan asked.

Kruger pointed at the phone. "I've gotten calls from the Prosecuting Attorney, three county commissioners, and every media outlet within a hundred miles. Overman has a lot of juice, and this thing has taken on a life of its own. We need results."

"Are you giving us permission to bring the spook in for a sit-down?" Brannigan asked.

Kruger looked at him. "Absolutely."

CHAPTER THREE

Nick and Felicia walked along Seabreeze Avenue after having lunch at Johnny Longboat's. Nick sensed that Felicia was bothered by the visit from the police and tried to get her focused on something more pleasant. The street was a steady stream of cars hustling to get from where they were to where they weren't.

"Now you see why I like The Keys," he commented. "No one's ever in a hurry down there."

Felicia chuckled. "Yeah, it's pretty laidback. That's why I like it, too."

"If I ever get the urge to move up here, smack me."

"You got it, tough guy."

He wrapped his arm around Felicia's waist and pulled her close. "Did you enjoy lunch?"

"It wasn't bad, but I remember why I don't care for Florida lobsters."

"Why?"

"Too scrawny, not enough meat."

"Sounds like a few women I used to date," Nick cracked.

Felicia giggled. "I'm not gonna ask you to explain that one."

"I always said you were smart."

They entered an antique store and milled about, looking over the high-priced goods. Felicia picked up an ornate art deco candelabrum and examined it. "What do you think of this?"

"It's lovely. What is it?"

She gave him a disapproving look. "Cute."

After visiting a few more shops, they walked back to the hotel.

"Want to hit the beach?" Felicia asked.

"Only if you wear that string bikini that always gets me hot."

She gave a sultry laugh. "Just so happens I packed it, tough guy."

They entered the lobby and were immediately approached by Brannigan and Cortez. Nick eyed them with suspicion. *Aw, shit. Now what?*

"Mr. Seven," Brannigan began, "would you mind coming with us?"

"Why?"

"We have some more questions."

"Where you takin' him?" Felicia demanded.

Brannigan handed her a business card. "We'll try to have him back by bedtime."

Nick looked at Felicia. "Call my attorney. Tell Grand everything that happened and have him meet me there." He glanced at Brannigan and Cortez. "ASAP."

Nick sat at a table in the interrogation room with his hands folded in his lap and his jaw clenched, staring straight ahead at the wall. He knew what the detectives were about to do, but twelve years of dealing with terrorists and bureaucrats can condition you to take anything. Brannigan sat opposite him, sipping coffee, while Cortez leaned his wiry frame against the wall with his hands shoved into the pockets of his trousers.

"Ya know, Seven," Brannigan began, "I can't say that I really blame you for this. You've got a hot babe with you, a great life in the Keys, then someone like Kristine Overman jumps up out of your past and bites you on the ass. Might tend to make things uncomfortable for you, wouldn't it?"

Nick gave him an amused look but remained silent. *How the hell did a moron like you ever pass the civil service exam?*

"Owning a bar seems like an odd career choice for a former spy," Brannigan continued. "How did you get into that line of work?"

Nick didn't respond, but mentally counted to ten while wondering when his lawyer would show up to rescue him from this drivel.

"What else do you do in Key Largo, Seven?" Cortez asked. "Ever do a little moonlighting, like private security or being a leg breaker for a loan shark? Guy like you has the right qualifications."

Nick stared straight ahead. *You might as well break out the rubber hoses because I'm not talking.*

"Those Overmans sure have a lot of money," Brannigan observed. "Wouldn't mind getting my hands on some of that loot. Maybe your business isn't doing as well as you'd like and you wanted to expand or remodel. A large infusion of some of that cash would come in handy. Is that what happened? Did you hit up Overman for a loan and he turned you down, so you decided to take it out on his kid?"

Nick glared at him. *Is everyone around here as stupid as you?*

Brannigan leaned forward and rested his arms on the table. "You seem like an intelligent guy, so let me lay this out for you. Our problem with your story is that you can't prove where you said you were when the girl was killed. I mean, sure, your girlfriend said she left you there when she went inside to powder her nose, but what would you expect her to say? She's gonna back your play, right?"

"You might as well give it up, Seven," Cortez said. "We'll find a witness that places you on the observation deck with the girl. When we do, it's all over."

Nick took a deep cleansing breath then slowly exhaled. He held his hands in the air. "Okay, guys, it looks like you've got me, so here's what happened. Kristine and I argued in the bar, she tried to hit me and I stopped her. I was pissed so I followed her outside, dragged her to the top deck, strangled her and threw her overboard. Then I felt terrible remorse for what I did and jumped into the ocean to bring her body back to the boat so I could hide it somewhere while I made my getaway. Are we happy now?"

Kruger entered the room with a distinguished-looking man in his sixties with silver hair and a deep tan, wearing a light gray suit, white shirt and stylish maroon tie. Nick exhaled in relief when he saw his attorney, G. Rand "Grand" Logan.

"This is Mr. Seven's attorney, Mr. Logan of Miami," Kruger said.

"Is my client a suspect?" Grand asked.

"Right now, he's a person of interest," Kruger replied.

"Are you formally charging him with anything?"

"Not at the moment."

"What does that mean?" Grand pressed.

"It means this is an ongoing investigation and we aren't prepared to share anything more at this time."

"Then this interview is over. Come along, Nicholas."

Nick and Grand left the precinct and got into a waiting limo. Once they were underway, Grand opened the mini-bar and poured two glasses of scotch. He handed one to Nick then relaxed in his seat, losing his courtroom bluster.

"Good to see you again, Nick."

"I wish it were under better circumstances."

"If there were better circumstances you wouldn't need my services, would you?" He sipped his drink. "Let's get around the elephant in the room. Did you do away with J.P. Overman's youngest offspring?"

Nick looked at him for a moment. "No, I did not."

"I didn't think so but I had to ask. What happened on The Gold Flamingo last night?"

"Felicia and I went out there to have some fun. While I was at the bar Kristine Overman approached me, we exchanged a few unpleasant words, she tried to smack me, I stopped her, and she swore she'd get even with me."

"Get even with you for what?"

"She claimed it was because I dumped her, but any spark we may have had fizzled a long time before that. I felt it was time to move on."

"How long since you'd seen her?"

Nick thought. "About six years. I didn't really keep track."

"Go on."

"About a half-hour later I was on the deck outside, alone, when I heard a commotion and someone screaming from the observation deck, two stories above. I looked over in time to see a body going overboard, and I dived in to save whoever it was. I didn't know it was Kristine until I was back on board."

"Interesting," Grand mused. "Did anyone see you outside the casino?"

Nick shook his head. "Not that I'm aware of. Felicia had gone inside a few minutes earlier, and I didn't see anyone else hanging around."

"How did Miss Overman take your decision to break things off?"

Nick smirked. "She was a spoiled rich girl who wasn't accustomed to hearing the word *no*. How do you think she took it?"

Grand chuckled. "I can imagine. That's why I never made that mistake with my own children. Tell me about this argument you had at the bar."

Nick took a sip of his scotch while recalling the events of the previous night. "She started in with a bunch of trash talk about Felicia, mainly about her ethnicity, then went into this rant about how I dumped her, and she was going to get even with me for it. She said that nobody walks out on her, and I should watch my ass because I'd get mine someday."

"How did you react to all of that?"

Nick looked at him. "I resisted the urge to punch her lights out, but it wasn't easy."

Grand laughed. "Thank God you had self-control. Was that exchange typical?"

Nick slowly shook his head. "Not from what I remember. To be honest, I was a little surprised when she went off on me like that."

"What else do you know about the Overman clan?"

"J.P. got his money the old-fashioned way, by inheriting his father's millions and increasing them ten-fold. Never did an honest day's work, and made a career out of stiffing any-one who worked for him. Kristine was the youngest of three kids. There was a sister named Brittany who died of a drug overdose a few years ago and she has a brother, J.P. junior, who inherited his old man's nasty personality. J.P. senior lives in Bal Harbour with Mrs. Overman number two, and his first wife has an overpriced bungalow on Palm Beach Island. You can piece together the rest from the society pages."

"Yes, the Overmans are very well known in certain circles. How did you get along with the rest of the family?"

Nick took a sip while composing a tactful response. "Let me put it this way. If you thought Lincoln made an error in judgment when he signed the Emancipation Proclamation, you'd get along great with that crowd."

"How did you and Kristine get together in the first place?"

"She was in Cricket's one night when a drunken customer got out of hand. The guy took a swing at me, I threw him out, and the next thing I knew, Kristine was on me like a sweat-shirt in July."

"Just out of curiosity, why did you date her?"

Nick thought for a moment. "She was very pretty, and I

wasn't seeing anyone at the time. She could make nice when she wanted, but *nice* only went skin deep. I'd read about her family in the tabloids but after a while, I found out that those stories were just the tip of the iceberg."

"How so?"

"I've bagged terrorists who had better table manners. Am I in serious trouble?"

"I don't think so, but I'd feel better if we could come up with a witness to verify your story. What did the police glean from their interrogation?"

"Just my name, rank and serial number. There's one thing they said this morning that may be helpful. They said they weren't certain if she was dead before or after she hit the water. Any way to get hold of the M.E.'s report when it's completed?"

"I can file a motion for discovery, but only if they decide to charge you with the crime. You realize that J.P. Overman isn't going to let this sit idle."

Nick laughed softly. "Yeah, he knows how to spread his money around to get what he wants. He's also got the subtlety of a suicide bomber. Add in the fact that he never liked me, and we've got an uphill battle. What's the plan?"

"Don't talk to the police without my being present. As to witnesses and possible motive, I have investigators who can look into this." He finished his drink. "I think I have all I need for the moment. May I drop you at your hotel?"

"Yes, please. Felicia's probably going frantic by now."

Grand smiled. "How is that charming girl?"

"Worried. Otherwise, fine."

"Tell her to put her fears to rest. You didn't commit this heinous crime and we're going to prove it."

Nick entered his suite and was immediately greeted by Felicia. She gave him a comforting embrace and rested her cheek on his chest. He ran his hand along her shoulder.

"You okay?" she asked.

"Yeah. No rough stuff this time."

"Did Grand find you?"

"Uh-huh. We had a little talk after he got me away from the cops."

Nick walked her to the balcony and they sat down in the cushioned wicker chairs.

"What happened?" Felicia asked.

"More of the same. They made it clear that they think I did it, and said if I confessed, it'd go a lot easier on me."

"The cops aren't lookin' at nobody else?"

"If they are, they're keeping it a secret. I know Grand's investigators will check this out, but I have to do something."

"Like what?"

He looked at her. "Return to the scene of the crime."

CHAPTER FOUR

The water taxi from the Sailfish Marina easily cut through the mild chop of the Atlantic, its flags ruffling in the breeze. A couple dozen passengers milled about, some taking pics of the passing scenery. When the boat eased up to the taxi dock on The Gold Flamingo, Nick and Felicia made their way to Rock Bianco's office.

"Rock, I'd like you to meet Felicia Hagens," Nick began. "Felicia, this is the infamous Rock Bianco I've told you so much about."

Rock smiled politely and delicately shook Felicia's hand. "I'm pleased to meet you."

"Pleased to meet you, Mr. Bianco."

"Call me Rock." He looked at Nick. "What's up?"

"The cops are convinced I killed the Overman girl and it seems they're not looking at anyone else. Since they won't exonerate me, I need to do it myself."

"What do you need?"

"I'd like to look at whatever your eyes in the sky captured last night."

Rock picked up the phone and called his head of security, telling him that Nick was to be allowed access to the video surveillance room.

"It's on the third floor. When you're done, why don't you two join me for dinner?"

"We'd be glad to."

Nick and Felicia entered the secured area on the third deck. The room was a maze of color monitors, with a dozen people intently watching the action on the screens. Each observer wore a Bluetooth ear piece to communicate with the floor-walkers if they saw anything suspicious. A young man in a short-sleeved shirt and wire-rimmed glasses approached.

Nick indicated the monitors. "Tell me how this works."

"These are all live feeds and each one is saved in a file on the server mainframe."

"What if someone wanted to see the action from a specific date and time?"

"I key it in and pull it from the file. If you need a hard copy, I can burn it onto a CD-R or thumb drive. What are you look-ing for?"

Nick recalled the timeframe of everything that had hap-pened. "The promenade deck casino bar area last night, be-tween nine and ten, and the observation deck from nine-thirty to ten. Do you have cameras outside each casino?"

"Of course."

"Then add the area outside the promenade casino, starting at nine-thirty."

"Can you be more specific?"

Nick examined a large diagram on the wall illustrating each floor on the boat. He placed his finger on a spot outside the casino. "This is where I was standing."

The man moved to a keyboard, then his fingers flew over the keys. "Give me a few minutes."

Ten minutes later he handed Nick three discs, all labeled. Nick and Felicia took seats at a vacant monitor and Nick in-serted the disc from outside the casino. He hit the fast-for-ward button then played it. He pointed at the images.

"There we are, standing at the railing, and there you go in-side." He noted the time. "Right where I said I was."

They continued watching. After Felicia went inside, Nick stood at the railing, looked up when his attention was cap-tured by the commotion from the upper deck, then took off his jacket and dived overboard. A couple of minutes later, Felicia reappeared, looked over the railing, grabbed Nick's jacket then ran toward the steps that led to the taxi landing.

Nick replaced the disc with the one from inside the casino. The video showed him seated at the bar, Kristine Overman approaching him, and her attempted assault and argument, followed by her quick departure. Nick hit the pause button as something caught his eye. He pointed at a figure on the screen.

"Look at the guy seated at the roulette table. As soon as Kristine marched past him, he got up and followed her."

"You recognize him?"

"No. Let's see what happened up on the roof."

He replaced the disc with the one from the observation deck camera. It had a limited view and the first part only showed the roof of the casino and the ocean. Nick fast forwarded until two figures appeared. It showed Kristine Overman slowly backing up to the railing then being approached by a man. He looked to be average height, with dark hair, wearing a light-colored jacket. They stood for a couple of minutes and appeared to be having a heated argument, each one gesturing forcefully at the other. The man abruptly drew back his left hand, backhanded Kristine across the face, delivered two more forceful slaps then moved in closer. She returned his slaps then punched him in the chest with her fists. He grabbed her wrists but Kristine continued struggling. He wrapped both hands around her throat and proceeded to strangle her. Kristine's hands instinctively went to his in an effort to break free, but she went limp and her head fell backwards. The man bent down, grabbed her by her ankles then flipped her overboard. He quickly departed with his face cast down.

"Wow," Felicia softly uttered. "Nick, I hate to say this, but from the back and in that light, that kinda looks like you."

"You noticed that, too?"

He rewound the scene then played it again in slow motion, making mental notes. *He struck her with his left hand but it was involuntary, not an intentional cover because he was obviously enraged. I wish there was audio so I knew what they were arguing about. The jacket he's wearing could be white, or light tan. The light's so poor I can't really tell.*

When the scene was finished, Felicia spoke. "What does this prove?"

"The one from outside the casino proves I was there when the murder went down. I wonder if the cops looked at this?"

"From what you said, they're too busy lookin' at you."

"You got that right."

Nick gathered up the discs then spoke to the technician.

"Did a couple of Fort Lauderdale police detectives ask you for copies of last night's action?"

He consulted a clipboard. "Yeah. They wanted a dupe from the observation deck, the same times you asked for."

Nick's brow furrowed. "Nothing else?"

The man shook his head. "That's it."

Nick escorted Felicia to the dining room on the first floor, where they found Rock seated at his private table. Rock stood when they approached, held Felicia's chair for her, then resumed his seat.

"You find anything?" he asked.

"Yeah. I need to borrow these discs."

"Keep 'em."

A server came to the table and they placed their orders. The dining room ambience was a cut above the standard casino offering, with comfortable furnishings, subdued lighting and background music, and a soothing nautical theme.

Nick looked around the nearly full room. "You've done all right out here, Rock."

He shrugged. "Tourists. They see legalized gambling and they think they'll win enough to pay for their trip."

"You don't turn a profit?" Felicia asked.

"I do okay, especially when there's a convention in town. The church groups are the best. Those holy rollers say a few Hail Mary's and hope they'll strike it rich."

Nick laughed. "Yeah, but how much of it actually makes its way into the collection plate on Sunday?"

"I detected a West Indies accent in your voice," Rock said to Felicia. "Are you from Jamaica?"

"Barbados," Felicia replied.

"Beautiful island. I've spent a few vacations there." He took a long swallow of whiskey. "How did you happen to come to the States?"

"My father's a retired Marine Colonel and he moved there after he mustered out. That's where he met my mom. After high school I came here to live with an aunt so I could join the corps. When my hitch was up, the CIA came callin'." She jerked her thumb in Nick's direction. "That's where I met this tough guy."

Rock gave a gruff chuckle. "Nick, you've been holding out on me."

Nick smiled. "You're a professional gambler. You know you never show your hole card."

Rock raised his glass in a toast. "Good point."

Their orders arrived. Nick noted the elegant presentation of grilled salmon on a leaf of romaine lettuce, accompanied by roasted vegetables and red-skinned potatoes, all finished off with a fancy garnish. *I need to pass this along to my kitchen manager when I get home.*

They continued their small talk over the course of the meal, covering everything from fishing to the demands of the tourist trade. Nick surmised that Rock was enjoying showing off his well-hidden classy side to his guests. *I've seen him bareknuckle the hell out of someone he caught cheating at the tables, but he knows when to turn on the charm.*

Rock indicated the discs Nick had set on the table. "Did

those tell you anything?"

"One of these established my alibi at the time of the murder. Did you talk to the cops last night?"

Rock shook his head. "Told 'em I was too busy. Why?"

"Your tech guy told me they only wanted to see the video from the murder scene. They didn't ask for the casino footage."

"I'm curious," Felicia said. "If the girl's killin' was bein' recorded, how come your people didn't catch it and try to stop it?"

"Their focus is on the casinos, where the action is," Rock said. "They're watching for pickpockets or someone who might be cheating, like counting cards at blackjack, or communicating with an accomplice on their phone. About the only thing that gets their attention from outside is an unauthorized boat or someone trying to sneak on board without going through security." He addressed Nick. "Sounds like the cops really think you killed that broad."

"It seems to be the popular opinion."

Rock sipped his drink. "Anything I can do to help?"

"Yeah. My attorney has P.I.'s looking into this. They'll want to come out here, look the place over, talk to any potential witnesses. Is that a problem?'

"Not for you. Tell them to call me first."

"I appreciate it."

They finished dinner, exchanged pleasantries then prepared to leave. When Nick and Felicia were on their way out of the room, she spoke.

"He don't seem so tough to me."

"Just don't let him catch you cheating."

It was a typical Fort Lauderdale beach evening, marked by couples and small groups sitting in cabana chairs near the water's edge, nursing cocktails and carrying on semi-private conversations. The background music from the nearby water-front clubs was a blend of everything from soft rock to Ca-lypso, with a dash of Country added for seasoning. A variety of food aromas drifted in from the outdoor grills and beach-front restaurants.

Nick and Felicia walked hand in hand, barefoot along the water's edge, the incoming tide washing over their feet. They had both changed into swimwear after returning from the boat. Nick wore an open box-cut shirt that allowed the gentle breeze to keep him cool. He glanced at Felicia's hips swaying ever-so-sexily under the white mesh throw she wore over her string bikini.

They hadn't said much about their fact-finding trip or the day's earlier events. Nick was irritated about being the prime suspect in a crime he didn't commit, and he knew Felicia was upset, too. When they returned to shore after dinner he had suggested the moonlight stroll as a distraction.

"So pretty and peaceful out here," Felicia said. "I always liked walkin' along the beach back home at night, listenin' to the tides roll in."

"Do you ever get homesick?"

"Once in a while, 'specially around holidays and birth-days."

"Any regrets about staying here instead of going back there?"

She stopped and looked up at him. "None. Any regrets about askin' me to stay when that job was finished?"

Nick cupped her cheek with his palm and gazed into her soft eyes. "Not a one. Why would I have second thoughts about making you a part of my life?"

Felicia shrugged. "I thought maybe you had a pretty full agenda, and I wasn't sure I'd fit into it."

Nick leaned down and planted his lips on hers, giving her a gentle kiss. "Life was nothing before you came along. Just an endless parade of meaningless encounters."

They looked out at the ocean. The lights of a cruise ship crossing on the horizon broke up the endless darkness. Seagulls pecked at seaweed that had washed ashore. Sounds of laughter from a nearby group who were clearly enjoying themselves drifted in, along with the unmistakable aroma of reefer.

"I could almost get a contact high from that group if we stand here long enough," Nick joked.

They continued walking further down the beach.

"Since you brought it up," Felicia said, "can I ask you somethin'?"

"What did I bring up?"

"Your life before we reconnected a few years ago."

Nick felt his gut clench a bit. Revisiting his past wasn't something he liked to indulge in very often, preferring to let sleeping ghosts lie. There were enough of them to occupy the world's largest haunted house at Halloween. He had worked hard at putting that unpleasantness in a vault under double lock and key, with instructions not to open it. He also realized that Felicia was now an integral part of his life, he trusted her, and part of that trust involved candor, no matter how uncomfortable it was.

"Such as?"

"This girl they think you killed."

"What about her?"

"You tell me. Were you two very close?"

"Not really."

"How long did you date her?"

"A few months."

Felicia stopped and looked at him. "Okay, Mister Tightlips. This is me you're talkin' to, not some board of inquiry where you stick to the facts and nothin' but."

Nick twirled a strand of her long hair that blew in the

breeze. "I'd characterize my relationship with Kristine Overman as a one-night stand that turned into a runaway train heading for a fork in the tracks. Came a point where I had to decide whether to stay on board or jump off."

"How did you find yourself on that train in the first place?"

"She showed up at Cricket's one night with a few friends. I think they were on their way back from Key West. One of the other customers clearly bagged his limit and when we cut him off, he got loud and nasty. I told him to leave, and he took a swing at me. You can guess the rest."

Felicia giggled. "Reminds me of times back home. Then what?"

"She dumped her friends and hung around for the rest of the evening. We started spending time together, nothing serious, until I finally had enough."

"You said the other night how that kind of life wasn't for you, but why did you hang out with her in the first place?"

Nick looked at her. "Maybe I was bored, and there wasn't anyone else around at the time. When she told me who she was, I was also a little curious about her family and wanted to see if the stories I'd heard were true."

"Were they?"

"Let's just say I saw enough to convince me that my way was better."

She squeezed his hand while peering into his eyes. "Which way was that?"

"Calling my own shots."

She hugged him and rested her head against his chest. Nick returned her embrace, running his palm over her shoulder and inhaling her soft, sexy scent. He put his fingers under Felicia's chin, gently tilted her face upward, then kissed her. She returned his passion, teasing him with her tongue. Nick was lost in the moment and didn't notice a large wave that crashed ashore until it washed over their legs, nearly knocking them over. He pulled back slightly and looked into her eyes.

"Did you cause that?" he teased.

Felicia laughed softly. "I was gonna blame you for makin' the earth move, tough guy."

He took her hand and led her back to the resort. They went to the outdoor Tiki bar and ordered drinks, then took them to a table.

"Now it's your turn," Nick said.

"My turn to do what?"

"Tell me about life on Barbados before you came here."

Felicia took a drink. "You sure you want to hear about that? It's kinda borin', really."

"Oh, come on, Felicia. There must be one story you've been dying to tell me."

She was silent for a moment. "Okay, here goes. You knew I was workin' as a bouncer in a waterfront saloon, right? It was a dive called Stinky Dick's."

Nick laughed. "Seriously?"

She raised her palm. "Swear to God. Not one of the places on the tourist maps, but the sailors and charter boat crews made it their local hangout. One night, a waitress told me that one of the sailors in a group on shore leave made a bet with his buddies that he'd hook up with me."

Nick continued chuckling. "No way."

"It gets better. This guy pestered me all evenin', makin' excuses to talk to me, usin' every lame come-on he could think of. Finally, to get him off my back, I gave him a phone number and said I'd show him a good time if he called me after I got off work." She sipped her drink. "It was the number for the local police precinct."

Nick burst out in laughter. "That's beautiful!"

Felicia laughed along with him. "I could just picture his face when they answered the phone and he asked for the hot babe from Stinky Dick's who promised to light his fuse."

Nick squeezed her hand as his laughter subsided. "Felicia, I'm sorry."

"For what?"

"This whole thing we've gotten into. When I suggested coming up here for a few days, it was so we could enjoy a change of scenery."

"Hon, it's not your fault this happened. In spite of this mess, I've had a really good time."

"You have?"

"Of course. I got to spend a few days with you at a beach resort with people waitin' on us, I had a spa treatment, and we found some terrific food. Plus, your friend Rock is a real hoot. What's not to like?"

Nick smiled. "Thank you."

CHAPTER FIVE

The exclusive community of Bal Harbour is located on the northern tip of the barrier island commonly known as Miami Beach. Established in 1947, it has a mean population of less than 3,000, mostly people of wealth. Many of the homes are situated on the ocean, and property can run into the millions.

The late morning sun highlighted the various varieties of palm trees, reflecting off their waxy fronds. Brannigan slowed the Ford sedan to a stop in the circular drive in front of J.P. Overman's seaside mansion. He and Cortez got out and looked over the spread-out two-story white stucco structure with an orange tiled roof. The house itself wasn't much, slightly smaller than Graceland but without the southern charm. The extensive grounds were immaculately manicured and adorned with palm trees, hibiscus bushes and cypress trees.

Brannigan jerked his thumb at a black lawn jockey near the front door. "Nice touch."

"Who the hell keeps something like that in front of their home, especially in southern Florida?" Cortez asked.

"We're about to find out." Brannigan took a deep breath, then pressed the doorbell. "This is one part of the job I hate — talking to the family after something like this."

The door was opened by a butler who took them to Overman's private study at the rear of the ground floor. Sunlight streamed in through the floor-to-ceiling windows. The room was decorated with antiques, oil paintings and red leather chairs. Overman stood behind his mahogany desk, gave a courteous smile and shook hands with them. He was of average height, slight of build, with a full head of dark hair streaked with wisps of gray that confirmed his sixty-odd years. He wore a blue blazer over a white open-necked shirt. He emitted the air of someone who didn't tolerate fools or bullshit.

"Thank you for seeing us, Mr. Overman," Brannigan began as they sat down. "We understand this is a difficult time and we'll try to be brief."

Overman sat in a padded swivel chair. "Anything I can do to help you apprehend the person responsible."

Cortez took out his note pad and a pen. "We spoke with three of your daughter's friends who were with her the other night. They said it was her idea to visit the Gold Flamingo. Any idea why she chose to go there?"

Overman stared at him before responding. "I don't see what that has to do with anything, Detective."

"It's just that there are a lot of night spots in Fort Lauderdale and Miami. Why pick that one?"

"I have no idea, and I didn't keep her social calendar. I understand you have a suspect in mind."

"We've identified a person of interest," Brannigan replied.

"How did you know?"

"I have my sources," Overman said. "I also know who this person of interest is, so let's cut the crap and talk about him, shall we?"

"Fine," Cortez said. "What can you tell us about Nick Seven?"

Overman snorted in disgust. "That thug? He's nothing more than a paid assassin, a human blight."

"Personal feelings aside," Brannigan said, "we understand he and your daughter used to see each other. Anything you can tell us about that?"

Overman rested his elbows on the arms of his chair and placed his fingertips together in front of him. "Against my better judgment, my daughter was convinced she wanted a relationship with him. I had him checked out and didn't like what I found. I tried to talk her out of it, told her what she was getting involved with, but she didn't care. When I couldn't convince her that Seven wasn't worthy of her, I kept silent. I thought that after time passed, she'd see him for what he really is. Perhaps I should've insisted a little harder."

"It isn't always easy to tell your kids what's in their best interest," Brannigan commented.

"Do you have children, Detective?"

"Three daughters, all grown. I couldn't tell them anything, either."

"Then you see my dilemma. When it became obvious that she wouldn't listen to me, I allowed her to bring him to some of our social functions."

"What functions?" Cortez inquired.

"Our annual regatta, a fundraiser to save the manatees, that sort of thing."

Cortez made notes. "What was your impression of him?"

Overman paused. "He seemed impressed with the lifestyle my money could buy."

"Did you get the idea that he wouldn't mind having some of it?" Cortez asked.

"It crossed my mind."

"What about his interactions with your friends and business associates?" Brannigan asked. "Cordial, hostile, indifferent?"

Overman smiled. "Detective, my friends didn't get where they are by being foolish. They saw right through him."

"You said you did a background check," Cortez interjected. "What did you find out?"

"Aside from being a psychopath who was allowed to carry

a badge, I found out that he'd been married once. According to my sources, his wife was killed when he was working in England, but there was a hint that it didn't happen the way the official record indicated."

"Did your sources suggest that he may have been involved in a cover-up?" Brannigan asked.

"That was the conclusion I drew. You can understand why I was reluctant to let my daughter associate with him. Now we've seen the result."

"Did you share all of this with her?" Brannigan asked.

"Of course. Why are you asking?"

"Because we're having trouble coming up with a motive," Cortez answered.

Overman stared into his eyes. "He's a former spy. You know what kinds of things they get involved in, how many secrets they take to their graves. Obviously, he thought Kristine would talk about it. That's your motive."

"But their relationship ended a long time ago," Cortez said. "Why would he wait until now to do something?"

"That's for you to find out," Overman answered. "I only know that he cast my daughter aside when he took up with that barefoot wetback he's living with."

Brannigan glanced at Cortez and noted his lowered eyelids and tightening jaw. "Sounds like you've kept tabs," Brannigan said. "If he wasn't in the picture any longer, why would you do that?"

Overman gave a sly grin. "I didn't get where I am by being careless, Detective. I knew it was just a matter of time until he'd resurface. I wasn't about to let my guard down."

"The night your daughter was killed," Cortez said, "we found cocaine in her purse. Anything you can tell us about that?"

Overman looked at him. "It was obviously planted there, probably by that thug, to cast aspersions on her and take your focus off of him. Considering the scum he associates with, I'm sure he'd have no problem getting narcotics."

"She never had a substance abuse problem?"

"Absolutely not. I've already lost one child to that poison. I wasn't about to let it happen again."

"What about someone from her job?" Cortez asked. "Perhaps they could fill in the blanks on her friends or social habits."

Overman gave a small smile. "My daughter didn't have to work, Detective."

Brannigan stood. "I think that's all we need for the moment." He handed Overman a business card. "Thank you for your time. If you think of anything that may be helpful, please call us. We'll be in touch if we have any other questions."

Overman smiled benevolently. "I'm at your service any time."

They got into their car then left the estate.

"Not the most open-minded guy," Brannigan commented.

"No shit. That lawn jockey told us that."

"Ray, you didn't take what he said personally, did you?"

"Tell you the truth, I tuned him out after he used the word wetback. I don't think he has any use for anyone who didn't come over on the Mayflower."

"I think he has the world's biggest blind spot where his kids are concerned. Did you notice how fast he dodged the issue of the drugs in her purse?"

Cortez consulted his notes. "That thing he said about Seven's first wife. Think there's anything to that?"

"I'm sure he has people in D.C. who would've talked off the record. What about it?"

"He basically made him out to be a serial killer."

They rode in silence for a few minutes before Brannigan spoke. "What's your take—crime of passion or opportunity?"

"Crime of passion. Whoever did this didn't help

themselves to her purse, so that rules out robbery. It was rage, and very personal. There's one thing that still doesn't make sense."

"What?"

"Of all the hot spots to go partying, the girl picked Bianco's casino the same night her former boyfriend was there."

"What's your point?"

"Something brought these two people together that night in that place, and I'd like to know what it was."

"Coincidence isn't good enough for you? This may be a crime of passion, but opportunity was definitely in the room. Seven saw his and he took it."

Cortez shrugged. "Maybe, maybe not. What's next?"

"Back to the office. We need to do records requests on Seven, and get everything we can find."

Nick and Felicia checked out of their hotel that afternoon then made the two-hour drive to Key Largo, arriving home in the early evening. Nick called Cricket's to tell Raul, his manager, that they were back, and asked if anything had happened while they were away. After receiving a good report, he said they'd be in the following day. Nick saw the message light on the answering machine and played it back. When he heard the terse voice, he instantly became angry.

"Seven, this is J.P. Overman. Be at my home at nine o'clock sharp tomorrow morning. If you aren't there, I'll have some-one find you."

Nick punched the erase button. *Screw that.*

He walked into the darkened living room. Felicia had put some light Latin jazz on the stereo and lit a scented candle. She slinked toward him and draped her arms over his shoulders.

"This looks very cozy and romantic," he said.

Felicia caressed his cheek with her palm. "I thought we'd stay in since we're still on vacation. You okay with that?"

He kissed her. "Oh, yeah."

She stepped back, took his hands in hers, then pulled him into the middle of the room. Felicia began a slow dance, gently swaying her hips in time with the Bossa Nova beat. Nick picked up her cue. He wrapped one arm around her waist and put the other on her shoulder, then moved in rhythm with her.

"What brought this on?" he asked.

"You never take me dancin'."

He pulled her closer and got into their passionate embrace. Felicia rested her cheek on his chest and Nick inhaled the pleasing combination of musky cologne and her natural body chemistry. He moved his hand up to massage her neck under her long hair. Felicia purred softly and undulated against him while rubbing her palm along his shoulders. Nick felt a stirring in his groin the longer they danced, engaging in intercourse on their feet.

He tipped Felicia's head back slightly and kissed her on the cheek. She moved her lips to his and hungrily embraced them, letting her tongue do an exploratory mission into his mouth. Nick felt closer to her than he had in a long time and his arousal increased when Felicia rubbed against his crotch. She put her hand on the back of his neck and pulled his mouth closer, increasing the intensity of her kisses.

She danced him backwards to a bar stool and prompted him to sit, not breaking their passionate oral embrace. Nick pulled Felicia onto his lap and devoured her soft tasty lips. After a couple of minutes, she stood, then cupped his chin in her palm. The music changed to a slow salsa and Felicia's eyes seemed to take on a sultry glow.

Nick watched as she unbuttoned her shirt while

maintaining eye contact. She pulled her top aside to reveal her firm braless breasts, her nipples stiff with anticipation. Felicia swayed her hips in rhythm while unfastening her slacks. She teasingly pulled them down her legs, then kicked them off, showing her black lace thong. She leaned forward and let her hair fall about her face, then ran her long fingers through her mane and tossed her head back as she stood before him. She slowly ran her hands over her breasts then along her firm stomach while swaying with the music. Nick felt himself getting more aroused the longer she performed her sensual dance.

Coming closer, Felicia rested her open palms on his shoulders, then leaned in to tease his lips with hers while unbuttoning his shirt. She ran her fingers over his bare chest then down his torso until she reached his crotch. She gave him a lingering kiss while she unfastened his pants and pulled them down his thighs, letting his cock spring free.

Nick's heart beat faster as Felicia dropped to her knees, pulled his pants and shorts off then leaned forward to teasingly flick her tongue along the underside of his cock, causing him to jerk and throb. He took in a quick breath as her tongue traveled upward and her full lips engulfed him, pulling him into her mouth. He felt an involuntary moan of pleasure escape as Felicia expertly teased him.

She stood and turned, moving her full, firm ass in time with the music as she teasingly pulled her thong down her legs and then kicked it aside. She whirled to face him, her eyes radiating a look that said "I want you." Nick's gaze locked onto her curly trimmed pubic patch, moist with desire. She rested her thighs over his, settling onto his lap with his stiff cock standing straight between them. She maintained eye contact while undulating back and forth, teasing him.

Felicia placed her hands on his shoulders and gazed into his eyes while rubbing against him, increasing his desire.

Nick leaned forward to suck her engorged nipple into his mouth. Felicia emitted a soft moan while running her fingers through his thick hair.

"Oh, hon, you know that's the sensitive one."

Nick continued suckling her while she rubbed against him. He felt his desire increasing and took in a quick breath when her hand grasped his cock. She raised up slightly, then rubbed him along her smooth velvet lips. He felt her secretions lubricating him and heard her purr softly as she teased herself with his hardness.

"You like that, tough guy?" she asked. "You want to make love to your little island girl?"

Nick grasped her ass and panted. "Uh-huh. You're so damned hot."

Felicia lowered herself onto his stiff staff, her engorged lower lips embracing him with each downward thrust.

"Oooh, hon," she panted while taking him further inside. "Feels like you really want me."

"You know I do."

Felicia's tight wet sleeve embraced him. "How bad do you want me?" She stopped moving to clench her muscles against him, making him throb. "That much?"

Nick took in a quick breath. "You know what you're doing to me?"

"Mm-hmm. I'm drivin' you crazy, just like you do with me."

Felicia rocked slowly, agonizingly, increasing Nick's desire. He leaned forward to suck her breast and gently bit her hard nipple.

"Ooh, yeah, that's it," she said. "You make me tingle when you do that."

She moved a little faster. Nick slipped his middle finger between Felicia's cheeks, rubbing her while she rode him. She took in a sharp breath.

"Aw, damn, hon! You know what that does to me!"

Felicia rocked harder and faster against him, then gave a loud cry of pleasure when she climaxed, tightening around him. Nick thrust upward and swelled inside her when he had his own orgasm. She pulled his mouth off her breast, then kissed him hungrily while continuing to bounce up and down.

When their rapture finally subsided, Nick leaned back slightly and peered into her dreamy eyes. She cupped his cheek with her palm.

"*Eau a voce,*" she whispered.

"What does that mean?"

She kissed him. "Me and you."

Nick exhaled a satisfied breath. "Damn, girl, you're so good. What got into you this evening?"

Felicia gave a wicked chuckle while clenching her vaginal muscles around him. "Just showin' you how much I love you. Got a problem with that, tough guy?"

He kissed her. "I never will. I love you, too."

She ran her fingers along his sweaty cheek. "I kinda figured that out, but thanks for sayin' it anyway."

CHAPTER SIX

Nick scanned The Miami Herald the following morning, looking for any mention of the killing. He found a story reminding everyone that Kristine Overman, society's child from Bal Harbour, had been the victim of a brutal attack and that funeral services were pending. The article contained a quote from Captain Donald Kruger stating that his detectives were pursuing solid leads and an arrest was imminent. Another quote from J.P. Overman made it clear that he wouldn't rest until his daughter's killer was brought to justice. Also included was a quote from the Broward County prosecutor, who said, "No comment."

He tossed the paper aside then took Felicia to Cricket's. The lunch crowd looked good, judging from the nearly full parking lot. Felicia went behind the bar while Nick spent a few minutes talking with his manager, a young Cuban man named Raul. Nick poured a cup of coffee, then went to his office. He opened the door and immediately stopped.

J.P. Overman stood before him in his trademark Italian gray silk suit, red tie over a white shirt, and perpetual scowl. Overman possessed the warmth of a statue but not as much personality. His slate gray eyes bored into Nick's and when he spoke, it was in a tone laced with grandiosity and arrogance.

"How the hell did you get in here?" Nick demanded.

"You stood me up. I told you to be at my home at nine o'clock. I don't like it when people don't follow my instructions."

"And I don't like being bossed around by some two-bit Caesar in overpriced threads."

Nick breezed past him, took his seat in the swivel chair behind his desk, then leaned back and swung his legs up, crossing his feet on the corner. He took the cigar Rock Bianco had given him from his shirt pocket then searched his desk drawer for a book of matches. He lit it and took a few puffs to get it started.

Overman made a face. "Don't smoke in my presence."

Nick leisurely blew a cloud of smoke across the desk. "State your business in ten words or less."

"You killed my daughter and you'll hang for it."

"Nine words. I'm impressed. Care to tell me why I'd kill Kristine?"

"Greed. You wanted to get your slimy hands on my money and when she cut you off, you got angry."

Nick chuckled. "As usual, you've misstated the facts. It was my idea to break things off, and that was six years ago. As for your money, I don't need it or the bullshit that comes attached."

Overman looked at Nick as though he were something he had stepped in on the sidewalk. "Look at you. You're a hoodlum, a lowlife. You killed people for a living and you associate with criminals and street trash."

"Is your slate all that clean? That thousand-dollar suit doesn't cover up the dirt. How did you really amass all that wealth, J. P.?"

"That's Mr. Overman to you."

Nick chuckled. "Whatever you say, J. P." He took another puff. "Knowing how you operate, I'm sure you shared your stellar opinion of me with the cops."

"I told them what kind of vermin you are."

Nick nodded. "Uh-huh. Did they share any evidence that makes it look like I could've done it?"

Overman pointed his finger. "You either killed her, or you arranged for someone else to do it. There's no other possibility."

Nick slowly shook his head. "Leave it to a paranoid nutjob like you to turn this into a conspiracy. Why don't you focus that one-track mind on someone who might want to see Kristine dead? The list can't be that long."

Overman took in a deep breath for round two. "Seven, I could make things very unpleasant for you."

Nick's eyebrows arched. "How? By staying?"

"You have no idea how much hell I could cause to rain down on you. I personally installed most of the legislators in this state, not to mention the people who issue liquor licenses and operating permits."

Nick blew another puff. "I'm sure it was money well spent. What's your point?"

"They're all beholden to me. Unless you want to find yourself under a microscope, make a full confession and take responsibility for what you did."

Nick stared for a moment. "Blow it out your ass."

He observed Overman's face take on additional color, and he responded in a tone that matched his elevating blood pressure. His words were accompanied by his finger pointing for emphasis.

"You tossed my daughter aside so you could shack up with some island tramp from a shit country, then you killed her so she wouldn't expose your past. You have to pay for that."

Nick's eyes narrowed. "You're coming dangerously close to pissing me off, J.P. I'm a reasonable man, so here's my offer—you can take yourself and your racism the hell out of here under your own steam, or I can help you. What's it going to be?"

Overman glared at him for a moment. "Fine. I'll leave, but you haven't heard the last of this."

"I wasn't listening to the beginning of it."

Overman rapidly strode from the office, nearly knocking Felicia over on the way.

"Who was that?" she asked.

"The one and only J.P. Overman, father of the deceased."

"He gonna make trouble?"

Nick puffed the cigar. "Only if I let him."

The table in the Fort Lauderdale police department work room was covered with stacks of files, all bearing Nick's name. The records Brannigan had requested included everything from credit card statements to tax returns. He and Cortez had been navigating the paper maze for two hours.

Brannigan exhaled a weary breath. *Meticulous drudgery, sifting through mountains of paper in search of a clue. I should've taken my uncle's advice and become a bookie.* "You find anything?"

"Nothing much on his credit card statements and no odd calls on the phone bills," Cortez replied. "How about you?"

"According to the Monroe County Sheriff's office, Seven has four registered handguns and a permit to carry them."

Cortez tapped his pen on the desk. "I've been thinking of another angle. Wasn't Bianco mobbed up at one time?"

"That was the rumor but we've never seen anything unusual until this." He scowled. "Not for lack of trying."

"A little bad blood between you two, Phil?"

"Nothing worth rehashing."

"Didn't Seven say they had a history?"

"Yeah, he said he won his place in Key Largo from Bianco in a poker game." Brannigan leafed through the papers in front of him. "Here's the transfer of the deed. Looks like a straight deal, no record of any money changing hands. What're you thinking?"

"The initial M.E.'s report said there was cocaine in the

Overman girl's system and we found a couple of bags in her purse. Say Bianco knew about it and suspected she was dealing on his boat. A thing like that would jeopardize his gaming license. He has to eliminate the problem, so who does he call? His old pal who's trained in the fine art of killing and owes him a favor for basically handing over his business."

Brannigan mulled it over. "It's possible, but how do we prove it?"

"We start by talking to Bianco."

Brannigan smirked. "Good luck with that. I've dealt with him before. You'll get more cooperation from your chair."

"He has to talk to us since his boat's a crime scene, and he dodged us the other night." He propped one leg on the other and resumed tapping his pen. "What's the motive?"

"Are you back to that?"

"Humor me."

Brannigan reviewed the witness statements they had collected. "According to the bar patrons, Overman made some less-than-flattering cracks about Seven's girlfriend. Maybe he snapped."

"That's still pretty weak. Who else would have a good reason to want this girl dead?"

"If her old man wasn't in denial, we could ask him."

"Here's another thing. Why would Seven dive into the ocean to retrieve the body?"

"Easy — he had to create some kind of bullshit alibi since no one saw him where he said he was."

Cortez shook his head. "I don't buy that. If this guy was in the CIA, he's a stone-cold assassin, the kind who walks away after a kill."

Brannigan laid down the papers he had been reading. "Okay, let's play your game for a minute. You're Seven, you just strangled the girl and tossed her overboard. Your training tells you to walk away, like nothing happened, but something stops you from doing that."

"Like what?"

"Like somebody coming up to the observation deck. You hear people walking up the steps, maybe talking or laughing, and you know you're about to be discovered. What do you do?"

Cortez thought for a moment. "Kill the witnesses?"

Brannigan shook his head. "Too messy. You dive over and make it look like you're trying to rescue the girl. You'll be a hero and establish an alibi."

Cortez stared at him for a minute. "You saw the video. No one visited the observation deck until the uniforms went up there."

"No one admitted to being there before the patrol showed up. Big difference."

"What if it wasn't an alibi for him, but for someone else?"

"I'm not following."

"Seven had an accomplice who killed the girl, and he did his diving act to create a diversion so the real killer could get away. I'm sure he knows someone from the old days who'd do the job, especially if Bianco paid for it."

Brannigan shrugged. "It's possible."

"What about that other thing Overman told us, about Seven's wife?"

Brannigan held up a sheet of paper with numerous words blacked out. "Reading between the redactions, it looks like she was taken out by some terrorist Seven was after. Nothing here to indicate a cover-up like Overman hinted at."

Captain Kruger approached and dropped a file folder on the desk. "Coroner's final report. There were minimal amounts of water in the girl's lungs. She was dead before she was tossed overboard. Official cause of death is strangulation."

Cortez retrieved the file and scanned the contents. "This

also confirms there was cocaine in her system."

"Where are you going with this?" Kruger asked.

"Just a theory we're working on," Cortez answered. He looked at the autopsy photos and his brow furrowed. "Look at those deep cuts and bruises on her face. Someone was really out of control to do this much damage."

"The M.E. also noted an abrasion on the back of her neck, like a heavy chain had been torn off. Did you find anything like a necklace at the scene?"

"No," Cortez said.

"What have you found out about Seven?" Kruger asked.

"Quite a colorful background," Brannigan replied while looking through a folder. "According to his service record, this guy really got around when he was a spook. Served all over the world, racked up an impressive record, and won just about every citation they give out. He could've been a wheel but he chose to walk away. His record makes him out to be one tough son of a bitch."

"How did you get his service record?" Kruger asked. "I thought those things were classified."

"Our lucky day," Cortez answered. "Someone sent it to us anonymously."

"Who says nobody likes cops?" Brannigan cracked.

"Didn't I read that he has a woman from Barbados living with him?" Kruger inquired.

Brannigan consulted the file again. "Yeah, Felicia Hagens. She's a former spook, too."

"Tell me about this place he owns in Key Largo," Kruger said. "Anything there?"

"Not according to the records," Cortez said. "He's never been in trouble with the local authorities, and no complaints from any other agencies. His tax returns indicate that he turns a nice profit."

"I've known my share of bar owners down here. A lot of

those guys barely make ends meet unless they're doing business under the table. Is there anything to indicate that Seven could be involved in something besides the hospitality business?"

"Like drugs?" Cortez asked.

"I believe it could be a possibility, since the girl had a stash in her purse the night she was killed," Kruger said.

"Run with that for a minute," Cortez said.

"He owns a club on the Gulf with lots of traffic. He's pals with Rock Bianco, whose boat is outside the three-mile limit with no one watching him, and his girlfriend is from a country with loose banking practices. Does that give you a hint?"

Cortez referred to a sheet of paper. "His bank statements don't show any unusually large deposits, but the girlfriend could be using her connections to hide the cash there."

"Check it out. Did you talk with the girl's father?"

"Yeah, but he didn't have much to offer," Cortez said. "Most of his rant was about Seven. He made it clear they didn't get along and he's convinced he killed his daughter."

"Gentlemen, I suggest a road trip to Key Largo," Kruger said. "In the spirit of cooperation, call the local authorities before you go."

"We also want to talk to Bianco, since he blew us off the other night," Cortez added.

"Talk to the Pope if you have to," Kruger responded testily. "Just bring back something useful."

Nick and Felicia stood at the bar inside Cricket's, catching up on the latest Keys gossip with one of the servers. Nick had finally calmed down from Overman's surprise visit, and lost himself in catching up on paperwork that had accumulated during his mini-vacation. He tried to soothe his irritation by putting Overman's bluster in perspective. *He's arrogant, insecure, and a sociopathic bully. No wonder his kids are so screwed up.*

He felt Felicia's elbow nudge him in his side. She jerked her head toward the door.

"Looks like trouble just showed up."

Nick groaned and rolled his eyes when he saw Brannigan and Cortez, accompanied by his friend, Sheriff Ted Cain. They approached and Ted shook hands with Nick.

"Nick, I believe you know these two gentlemen," he said.

Nick stared blankly at them. "We've met."

"We have a few more questions," Brannigan said.

Nick led them to his private table on the outdoor deck and everyone took a seat.

"Sheriff Cain says you've never had any serious trouble here," Brannigan began.

"I guess I've been lucky," Nick said.

"Then why do you have so much artillery?" Cortez queried.

Nick looked at him. "You mean the guns I'm legally allowed to possess? Protection. I'm sure I don't need to quote the crime stats for an international vacation spot like this."

"Where do you keep these guns?" Cortez pressed.

"One here, one in my car, and two at home."

"Ever carry one on your person?"

"Not very often."

"So much for old habits," Brannigan commented. "We looked at your service record. Quite a list of accomplishments. You really could've gone somewhere in Spookland. Why give it up?"

Nick's eyes narrowed slightly. *How the hell did they get my file?* "I had enough and decided to quit. That's all I'm prepared to say on the subject."

"Tell us about your relationship with Rock Bianco," Cortez said.

"It's like I told you the other day. He used to own this club, I took it over, and we've stayed in touch."

"What other business do you two have going?"

"None. He runs his place, I run mine."

"He ever ask you for a personal favor?"

"Such as?"

Cortez hesitated for a moment. "Such as taking care of a problem on his boat, one that might put his gaming license at risk."

"I see Bianco socially when I go gambling once or twice a year. What kind of problem would he need my help with?"

"If he knew someone was dealing drugs out there, and he wanted them gone."

Nick's narrowed gaze returned. "As I said—he runs his place, I run mine."

"Do you ever have any problem with drugs here?" Brannigan asked.

Nick looked at him. "I screen everyone carefully before I hire them, and I keep my eyes open."

"If I can add something," Ted interjected. "Nick routinely asks us to run background checks on potential employees, and we've never responded to anything unusual."

"Is the background check standard practice for every bar owner in The Keys or a personal service?" Brannigan asked.

Cain's eyelids lowered slightly and his jaw tightened. Even his pencil-thin moustache seemed to be standing at attention. "I try to accommodate the local business owners whenever possible. I've found that it's had a positive impact. Perhaps you should institute something like that in Fort Lauderdale."

Nick bit his lip and suppressed a laugh. "Why the questions about drugs?"

"The Overman girl had cocaine in her system the night she was killed," Brannigan answered. "She also had some on her person. Any idea where she got it?"

"I wouldn't have a clue."

"There's something I'm stuck on that maybe you can help

me figure out," Cortez said. "You said you and Kristine Overman hadn't spoken in a few years. I just don't get how you two wound up on the same party boat at the same time. You're sure that wasn't planned?"

Nick stared at him for a few moments. "My answer hasn't changed since the last time you asked that question. I hadn't spoken to her in a long time, and I didn't know she'd be there the other night. Is there anything else you're having trouble processing?"

"Yeah, there is," Cortez said. "Your lady friend is from Barbados. You do any business there?"

"What business could I possibly have in Barbados?"

"How about banking? I hear the regulations are less restrictive than here."

Nick took a deep breath then slowly exhaled. *I could bring all this to a halt right now by turning over the surveillance video, but they'd bury it.* "I think I see where we're going. I don't have a bank account, a timeshare or half-interest in an ice cream stand anywhere in the West Indies." He stood. "If you'll excuse me, I have a business to run. You can see yourselves out."

Brannigan and Cortez left the club but Cain remained. "Why are the Fort Lauderdale police after you for that killing?"

"I guess they don't have anything better to do. Thanks for the testimonial."

"No problem." He hesitated. "You seem distracted. Something wrong?"

Nick paused a few seconds. "What those cops said about Kristine having coke in her system. I guess you never know someone as well as you think you do. The whole time we were going out, I never knew she used drugs. That might explain her behavior when she accosted me."

"Her actions were out of character?"

"She always had an air of self-importance but her comments never included threats or racial remarks. If she was buzzed, she might've felt feisty enough to pick a fight."

"You know that cocaine intensifies one's personality."

"And if you're an asshole to begin with . . ."

"What kind of relationship did you two have?"

"Strictly laughs and casual sex, nothing more. Have you ever worked with either of those guys before?"

"No. Why?"

"They seem eager to pin this rap on me and I'd like to know why."

"How many times have they interviewed you?"

"Today makes four."

"I'll admit that seems a bit excessive. I'll make some calls."

After he left, Nick went to his office to phone his attorney.

"Grand, I just had a visit from those detectives from Fort Lauderdale."

"Nick, I cautioned you about talking to the police without counsel."

"I didn't incriminate myself. They just showed up with the local sheriff, who's a good friend. They did share their newest theory, though."

"Which is?"

Nick laughed. "According to them, I'm now in the drug smuggling business. Kristine had cocaine on her person and they think I supplied it to her. They also wanted to know if I have any bank accounts outside the U.S."

"I get the feeling they're on a fishing expedition."

"Have your investigators come up with anything?"

"They've spoken with the personnel on duty that evening and verified your story about what happened in the casino, but none of them can corroborate your alibi. I'll pass along this new development. If drugs are involved, that may prove to be an alternate theory."

"Since they've come up empty, I found something you can use. I got the video surveillance from the night of the killing.

One of the cameras picked me up where I said I was."

"Excellent. Did you mention this to the police?"

"No, I thought it would sound better coming from you."

"Quite right, but let's do this correctly so you won't have any further problems. I'll arrange a meeting with the Broward County Prosecutor. In the meantime, try to keep a low profile."

Nick hung up then left the office. He approached Felicia. "Let's go home. I have a job for you."

CHAPTER SEVEN

Felicia sat at the computer in the den, reviewing the surveillance videos they had gotten from the Gold Flamingo. Nick had asked her to burn copies of the relevant portions showing what had transpired in the casino — him standing on the deck at the time of the murder and the murder itself. Her gaze was fixed on the screen as she edited the footage.

She froze the frame where Kristine was being strangled and looked intently at the woman, but not out of some morbid curiosity or satisfaction. Ever since the incident, her mind had been pre-occupied with why Nick had hooked up with the society diva in the first place. *He's the most down-to-earth, casual guy I've ever met. Whenever Nick had to wear a tux on an assignment, he hated it. I just don't see him mixin' with the caviar crowd. What was the attraction?*

She printed some still photos of Nick standing on the lower deck and of the man who followed Kristine out of the casino. She put the disc in a jewel case then took everything outside to the deck where Nick sat.

"Got it," she said while sitting down.

"Thanks. Maybe this will get the cops to back off."

Felicia stared into the horizon. "Ask you somethin'?"

"Of course."

"How serious were things between you two?"

"What happened to the *Don't ask, don't tell* pact we made when you moved in?"

Felicia manipulated the ruby cocktail ring on her right hand. "If you don't want to talk about it, that's okay, but it seems like someone's goin' to a lot of trouble to frame you. I'd just like to know why."

Nick took her hand. "The only thing between us was Kristine pissing off her old man."

"Why would she date you to get a rise out of her father?"

"Daddy issues. This was her way of thumbing her nose at the way he ran the family."

"Pretty strict?"

Nick smirked. "Arrogant and controlling to a fault. He spoiled all of his kids and drilled into them that the rules didn't apply to anyone named Overman. She was always doing things to get under his skin."

"Like what?"

Nick laughed softly. "One time, she dragged me to an opening at an art gallery on South Beach, some up-and-coming artist Overman was hot for. It was a semi-formal affair, and she showed up wearing something no self-respecting punker would be seen in. She'd even died her hair with pink and purple streaks."

Felicia laughed. "Sounds like quite a sight. What did her old man do?"

"After he vapor-locked, he pulled her off to the side and lit into her. I couldn't hear what he said, but he was gesticulating and making it clear that he wasn't amused."

"How did she react to that?"

"She smiled, shrugged, then went to the bar to get a drink. Does that paint a clearer picture?"

"Yeah. Thanks."

Nick closed his eyes and rubbed his temples with his fingertips.

"Another headache?"

"Starting."

Felicia stood behind him and placed her hands on his neck. "Put your head down." She massaged his neck and shoulders.

"You're stiff as a board. Why you lettin' this get to you so bad?"

"I don't like being in this position." He paused. "Now you know one of the reasons I got out of the spy racket when I did."

She continued her massage. "I thought it was because your wife got killed."

"That was part of it."

"What part didn't you tell me about?"

Nick was quiet for a moment. "At my last physical, the Doc noticed a propensity for migraines and high blood pressure. He said I was letting the job get to me."

She applied more pressure with her thumbs and felt his muscles relax. "What did you do about it?"

"What I always do—I ignored it."

"When are you gonna admit you aren't the same tough guy you were ten years ago?"

Nick put his hands on hers then turned to face her. "When you tell me I'm not."

She leaned over and planted a kiss on his lips. "You'll never hear me say that."

True to Nick's prediction, the Gold Flamingo had seen an increase in traffic since the night of the murder. Curiosity seekers who didn't normally frequent gambling establishments suddenly had an unquenchable desire to see the crime scene, driving the employees crazy with endless questions. Rock Bianco had spent his time ducking inquiries from the media, refusing to offer any comment while wishing the whole thing would blow over. He sat behind his desk, engrossed in paperwork. His paisley tie was loosened and the cuffs of his shirtsleeves were pushed up over his meaty wrists. His concentration was interrupted by knocking on the door.

"Come in," he called out.

Brannigan and Cortez entered the stateroom. Rock's gaze narrowed but he didn't bother standing to greet his guests, nor did he try to hide his contempt for anyone carrying a badge. "What?"

"We have a few questions, since you were too busy to talk the other night," Brannigan replied.

"Make it fast. I ain't got all day."

"What's your connection with Nick Seven?" Cortez asked.

"He's an old friend. We did some business together once."

"Yeah, we heard he beat you out of your bar in Key Largo in a poker game," Brannigan said. "I'm surprised a professional card shark like you would let that happen."

Rock shrugged. "Luck of the draw."

"Did you know that Kristine Overman had drugs on her the night she was killed out here?" Cortez abruptly asked.

Rock picked up the cigar that was burning in an ashtray, then blew a thick puff of smoke at them. "How would I know that?"

"Was she a regular customer?" Cortez asked.

"I don't take attendance."

"Come on, Bianco," he challenged. "A smart guy like you knows his clientele, especially the rich ones."

"What's your point?"

"If she was dealing out here, that would put your gaming license at risk. If it was my boat and I knew that kind of stuff was going on, I'd want the problem eliminated."

Rock's eyes narrowed. "What the hell are you gettin' at?"

"Just that I'd look for someone, say a trained killer who owed me a favor, who could make it go away."

Rock chuckled. "Is that the hot tip that brought you clowns out here?"

"Makes sense if you look at it from our side of the desk," Brannigan added. "You didn't get a dime for your place in

The Keys when Seven basically took it away from you. Maybe you thought he owed you one and you called in his marker."

Rock puffed his cigar and eyed Brannigan. "This ain't the first time you've tried to bust my chops, Brannigan. The last time was when you thought I was lettin' minors on board."

Brannigan scowled. "I remember."

"Remember the harassment complaint my lawyer filed with your Chief? How long were you on ass duty after that?"

Cortez cleared his throat. "What can you tell us about what happened the night of the murder?"

"Nothin'. I was hostin' a few special guests in my private room. I didn't hear about it until after it went down."

"Can any of those special guests verify your whereabouts?" Brannigan asked.

Rock looked at him for a moment. "Yeah. You can start with Judge Moretti."

"Judge Aldo Moretti of the Appellate Court?"

"That's the guy. If you don't believe him, try Sal Russo from the Prosecutor's office. He was here, too."

"Why would two upstanding court officers be in a huddle with a known gambler like you?"

"I believe there was some mention of a charity fundraiser for the Sons of Italy."

"I have to hand it to you, Bianco," Brannigan said. "You've really come up in the world, from the Vegas mob to rubbing elbows with the elite. There may be hope for you yet."

Rock stood. "If you have any more questions, call my lawyer. We're done."

Brannigan and Cortez left the office. Rock picked up the phone and placed a call to Nick.

"This is Rock. I just had a visit from those two dipstick cops from Fort Lauderdale."

"What did they want?"

He chuckled. "They think you killed that dame as a favor

to me because she was doing drugs out here. Can you beat that?"

Nick laughed along with him. "I like you, Rock, but not that much."

CHAPTER EIGHT

Broward County Prosecuting Attorney Frank McCorkle stood at an office window that afforded a view of the ocean. His gaze latched onto the numerous sailboats out for another day of fun in the sun. The vista was a stark contrast to his latest dilemma, one that could affect his future in politics if not handled carefully. In spite of the balmy morning weather outside, the atmosphere in the room was noticeably chilly. He had invited Captain Kruger, along with Detectives Brannigan and Cortez, to join him for his scheduled meeting with G. Rand Logan of Miami. McCorkle had dealt with the flamboyant attorney before, and wasn't looking forward to their latest face-to-face, especially when he heard why Logan wanted to see him. He turned to face his guests.

"You really think Seven came up with some miracle alibi?" Brannigan asked.

"According to his attorney, yes," McCorkle answered. "If he has, you've all been spinning your wheels the last few days, haven't you?"

"Wait a minute, Frank," Kruger interjected. "We had a solid lead and we followed it. Nothing else jumped up and bit us on the ass."

"For your sake, I hope you have a back-up plan," McCorkle said.

The door opened and Grand Logan entered, followed by Nick. After introductions were made, McCorkle began.

"What is this new evidence you've uncovered?"

Nick held up a DVD. "This is the footage taken by the

security cameras on The Gold Flamingo the night of the murder." He glanced at Brannigan and Cortez. "The complete footage, including the casino, not just the murder scene."

McCorkle gave Kruger a hard look, which he passed on to the two detectives.

"You want to know why nobody trusts the police?" Nick asked. "Because you guys couldn't find your ass with both hands and a GPS." He indicated a DVD player and television on the credenza. "May I?"

He inserted the disc. They all watched the initial confrontation between Nick and Kristine at the bar, followed by her abrupt exit. Nick hit the pause button.

"Look at the guy at the roulette table," he said. "He follows Kristine out of the room while I stay put."

"Who is he?" McCorkle asked.

"No idea," Nick said. He resumed playing the disc. The scene shifted to the area outside the casino, showing Nick and Felicia at the railing and Felicia going inside. Nick paused it again.

"That's from outside the Promenade Deck casino where I said I was. Take note of the time stamp." He resumed playing the footage of the murder itself then paused it. "If you notice the time on this one, it's the same as where I was, two floors below."

The room was shrouded in an awkward silence for several minutes.

"We'll need to verify these images," McCorkle said.

"Rock Bianco has the originals," Nick said. "If you ask him nicely enough, he might show them to you."

"Mr. Logan, I'm curious why you insisted on dealing with me personally instead of handing this over to the detectives."

"My client's interactions with the police haven't exactly been positive," Grand responded. "I'd like to point out that when he discovered this material, he wanted to get it into the right hands immediately. We could have given it to the media instead."

"I appreciate the consideration," McCorkle said. "It appears this office and the police owe you an apology, Mr. Seven."

"I trust there will be no more investigation of my client?" Grand asked.

"Unless something else turns up, you have my word."

Nick and Grand left. Kruger, Brannigan and Cortez stood to leave but were stopped by McCorkle.

"Just a minute, Captain. Why didn't your detectives find this?"

Kruger looked at the two. "That's a very good question. Phil, would you like to favor us with an answer?"

Brannigan shrugged. "We thought Seven was the guy, and you said Overman was piling on the pressure. We didn't think about checking all of the videos."

"Sloppy police work won't cut it in my jurisdiction, Detective," McCorkle reprimanded. "Since Seven did your job for you, I'd suggest you check out this other man in the casino, the one who followed the girl."

Brannigan took a step toward him. "Any time you think you can do my job better than me, say the word."

"Your job is to bring me evidence I can use to make good cases," McCorkle fired back. "You have no motive, no witnesses, and thanks to that security footage, your only suspect has an alibi."

Brannigan pointed his finger and was about to speak when Kruger held up his hand.

"That's enough," he interrupted sharply, then looked at the detectives. "You two get back to work."

"And I meant what I said about no more investigation of Seven," McCorkle added.

After the detectives left, Kruger looked at McCorkle.

"Now what?" Kruger asked.

"Now I have the unpleasant job of breaking the news to J.P. Overman," McCorkle said. "Who else are you looking at?"

"We're checking her friends and playmates, but it's a long list. So far, we haven't come up with anyone with a good reason to kill her."

"I read the M.E.'s report about drugs being in her system, and your officers found some in her purse. Anything there?"

"Not yet. Narcotics didn't have her on their radar, but we're still looking into it."

"Look harder, and keep me posted."

Cricket's was enjoying a brisk business that evening, thanks to a bachelorette party in one of the private rooms. The exterior deck was busy as well, with every table occupied. A break in the weather made it a perfect night for casual outdoor fun. Thirsty customers kept the wait staff busy while a local musician performed requests. Nick approached Felicia at the bar near closing time.

"Good crowd tonight," he commented. "How many pitchers of margaritas did that party go through?"

Felicia checked the tab. "Ten, plus a ton of appetizers."

"Girls gone wild," Nick cracked.

Raul approached. "Chief, can I ask you a favor?"

"Sure, amigo."

Raul leaned in close and lowered his voice. "I've got a date with one of the waitresses at Sharkey's. We been tryin' to get together for a week and her roommate's not gonna be home tonight. I was wonderin' . . ."

Nick grinned. "You were wondering if I'd take the money to the bank so you can keep your date?"

Raul chuckled. "Yeah."

"Get it ready then go have a good time."

"Thanks."

Nick was approached by a short man with dark curly hair, wearing glasses. "Excuse me. Are you Nick Seven?"

"That's right. Who are you?"

He handed Nick a folded document. "You've been served."

Nick quickly opened the document. His eyes narrowed and his hands trembled in anger He slammed it onto the bar.

"What is it?" Felicia asked.

"A wrongful death suit brought against me by J.P. Overman. Son of a bitch didn't waste any time."

"But you said the Prosecutor cleared you."

"That wasn't what he wanted to hear."

Felicia examined the paper. "Why is this guy comin' after you?"

Nick exhaled a deep breath. "If you figure it out, tell me."

Twenty minutes later Nick went to his car with the locked deposit bag. He noticed that the pole light near his reserved parking space was burned out. *Better get that fixed tomorrow. One more thing on my to-do list, right after get my ass cleared of this nuisance complaint.*

He took out his key fob and pressed the unlock button when he felt a sharp blow to the back of his neck that took him by surprise. He fell against the car, banging his head on the window. Nick reeled from the sudden shock but before he could regain his senses, his feet were kicked out from under him. He landed face down on the pavement. He tried to get up but was stopped by a hard kick to his stomach, and he doubled over in pain.

Nick lay face down and felt more kicks to his side, each one more powerful than the last, followed by fists raining down on his back. He tried to fend off the blows by folding his arms over his mid-section and curling up in the fetal position, but it didn't help. He felt blood running down his face when his head was forced onto the asphalt. After what seemed like an hour of being pummeled, Nick felt a sharp kick to his forehead followed by a man's voice saying, "Let's get outta here!"

Nick managed to lift his head in time to see three men running away. Through pain-soaked eyes he could make out that one of his assailants was wearing a blue and white windbreaker with a logo on the back. He tried to push himself up but decided it was hopeless. He collapsed on the ground, his head spinning and his heart racing. He panted hard and felt an upheaval deep in his gut. Nick propped himself up on his elbows and threw up. When his endless retching was over, he eased himself down, catching his breath. He reached around, found his keys and picked them up. He pressed the red button that set off the car's alarm, then let his hand fall to the ground.

He heard feet running in his direction. His head pounded as he swam in and out of consciousness. From out of the fog, he heard Felicia's voice saying "Get him inside!" Nick felt two sets of hands pulling him to his feet and helping him walk while he cradled his gut. He sat on a chair and focused his gaze on Felicia, whose face was etched with worry. *Now I've done it.*

"Are you okay?" she anxiously asked.

"Of course not," he muttered. "I just got the shit kicked out of me."

"I'm callin' Ted."

Nick grabbed her arm. "No cops. By the time they're done with this, it'll be me who attacked junior and the two Eagle Scouts who rescued him."

"Junior? You know who did this?"

Nick nodded weakly. "It was Overman's son. I recognized the name of the family yacht on the back of his jacket."

Raul handed him a glass of water. "You don't look so good, Chief."

Nick took a long swallow. "I don't feel so good. It's a matching set. Aren't you supposed to be on a date?"

"She'll keep."

"Thanks, amigo."

Felicia examined his injuries. "We need to get you to a doctor."

Nick waved her off. "Just get me home. I'll be okay."

Felicia and Raul helped him into the passenger side of the Mustang. Felicia drove them home. She walked him inside and eased him onto the couch.

He closed his eyes and rubbed his ribs. *Haven't taken a beating like that in years. Just shows how out of shape I am.*

Nick rested his head on the back of the couch and watched Felicia go to the bar in the kitchen. She poured herself a glass of scotch then took a long swallow. *I think I feel worse for her than I do for myself.*

She returned with a second glass and handed it to him. He took a sip then winced as the liquor irritated his raw throat.

"Think you can make it upstairs to bed?" she asked.

"Yeah."

Nick climbed Mount Everest to the second floor, then looked at his reflection in the mirror, eyeing the cuts on his face. *Someone's gonna wish tonight never happened.*

He sat on the edge of the bed while Felicia removed his shirt and performed some basic first aid.

"How come you let them jump you like that?" she asked.

"I didn't see it coming. The light over my parking space was out. Probably broken on purpose so those assholes could attack me. You gonna quit bitchin' on me anytime soon?"

"I'm worried about you."

Nick took her hand. "I know, and I appreciate it."

"I still think you should call the cops."

Nick shook his head. "Wouldn't do any good. Junior would have an alibi, bought and paid for."

Felicia finished patching him up. They both undressed and reclined on the bed. Felicia turned off the light and rested her hand on Nick's chest.

"The bag of money you were gonna deposit was still

underneath you when I got there," Felicia said. "Think they're pissed they didn't get it?"

Nick shook his head and felt his brain banging against his skull. "Nope. They didn't even try to make it look like a robbery. It was me they were after, and me they got."

"What're you gonna do about that lawsuit you got tonight?"

Nick exhaled a deep breath. "Worry about it in the morning." He leaned over and kissed her. "Go to sleep."

CHAPTER NINE

A bright burst of sun rays through the bedroom window and the squawk of seagulls trolling for breakfast in the nearby channel signaled daybreak. Nick awoke from a sound sleep but felt groggy. The bed was empty beside him and the aroma of coffee drifted up from downstairs. He stumbled to the shower and stayed longer than usual, the hot water soothing his sore muscles. He looked in the bathroom mirror while he dried off and noticed that his bruises were turning dark purple. The longer he stared at the results of his beating, the madder he got.

He dressed then went downstairs and joined Felicia on the deck. She poured him a cup of coffee from the carafe.

"You sleep okay?" she asked.

He eased into a chair. "Yeah. Thanks for patching me up last night."

"You're welcome. I'm just glad it wasn't any worse." She handed him a stack of photographs. "I got up early and printed those close-ups you wanted from the security cameras."

He looked at them while Felicia went inside to answer the phone. Something in the murder shot caught his attention. He stared at the close-up of the killer's hand, intrigued by the ring he wore. *Where have I seen that before?*

Felicia came from inside and handed him the phone. "It's Grand."

Nick took it. "Let me guess what you found waiting for you this morning—a civil suit filed by J.P. Overman."

77

"Very astute, Nicholas. I assume you were served as well."

"Yeah, last night. McCorkle must've broken the bad news to him. Can we counter-sue for harassment?"

"We could, but his battery of lawyers would wear you down before you'd see a penny."

"I don't want his money. I just want him to leave me alone. What's our next move?"

"My next move is to get my investigators to work proving your innocence. Yours is to stay put."

"I'm not going to sit here and do nothing. Another set of eyes always helps and I'm more familiar with the case."

Grand was silent for a few moments. "Just don't get too involved. We don't need any evidence getting thrown out for being tainted or illegally obtained."

Nick disconnected and set the phone on the table.

"What was that all about?" Felicia asked.

"His private eyes are going to look into this but I'm not waiting around." He picked up the picture he had been looking at and showed it to her. "Can you get a better close-up of this guy's left hand, the one he used to strike Kristine?"

Felicia examined the photo. "You interested in the ring he's wearin'?"

"Yeah. It looks familiar." He handed her another shot that showed the man following Kristine from the casino. "I need a clear close-up of this guy's face, too."

Felicia returned in a few minutes and handed him the enhanced pictures.

"That one of the guy's ring isn't real clear, but it's the best I could do."

Nick looked at it. "It looks like a medallion or crest."

"Looks like a sports ring to me, you know, like a World Series or Super Bowl ring." She sipped her coffee. "What next?"

"I'm going to see Rock. If this guy in the casino is a regular, maybe one of his floorwalkers knows who he is."

"Hon, you're not up to goin' anywhere right now."

"I can't sit around and do nothing."

Felicia paused a moment. "How about a compromise? We'll e-mail it to him and have him ask his guys if they recognize him."

Nick raised his coffee cup in a toast. "Good thinking, angel. You should do this for a living."

She shook her head. "Been there, done that."

She went inside to answer the ringing doorbell. Ted Cain joined Nick on the deck while Felicia stayed inside. He took a seat.

"To what do I owe the pleasure?" Nick asked.

"Just a courtesy call. I hear you had some trouble last night."

"My, what a big mouth grandma has."

"Grandma didn't call me. Raul did."

"There was no trouble, Ted."

Cain eyed him. "Uh-huh. How did you get those abrasions?"

"Cut myself shaving."

"Come on, Nick, talk to me. Attempted robbery?"

He shook his head. "It wasn't about the money."

"Do you know who did this?"

Nick hesitated. "Yeah, but I'm not pressing charges. Clear?"

"All right. Who was it?"

"J.P. Overman, Junior. He and two of his buddies did a tap dance on my ass."

"Why would Overman sic his son on you?"

"That's one thing about him — he likes to keep it in the family. He also filed a wrongful death suit against me for Kristine's murder."

Cain slowly shook his head. "Unbelievable. Why is he

coming after you?"

"Because I proved my innocence to the Broward County prosecutor and it wasn't what he wanted."

"That would explain the phone call I got from Overman before I came over here."

"What did he want?"

"He wanted to know why I was protecting a felon, since you're obviously guilty. He also implied that I was letting our friendship get in the way of my sworn duty."

"What did you tell him?"

"I reminded him that the murder didn't happen in my jurisdiction, and whom I choose to associate with is none of his damn business."

Nick laughed but winced at the pain it caused in his ribs. "Overman has a lot of connections, and he could make things difficult for you come election day."

"He pointed that out, but I ain't worried. Walk me through what's happened since the night of the murder."

Nick sipped his coffee. "Overman came to see me a couple of days after and accused me of killing Kristine. He said he'd see me hang for it."

"How did you get along with him when you were dating his daughter?"

"Strained is a good word. He didn't like me and I couldn't get all warm and fuzzy about him."

"Do you think he tried to influence the investigation?"

"I wouldn't put it past him. That's probably how those detectives got my service record. A lot of representatives in D.C. owe their jobs to him. Wouldn't take much to call in a favor."

"How did you square things with the Fort Lauderdale people?"

"By doing their job for them. Bianco gave me the video surveillance from the night of the murder. One of his cameras picked me up on the lower deck while Kristine was getting killed two flights up."

Cain paused for a few moments. "Why do you suppose the police didn't do a more thorough investigation and discover that on their own?"

"If I were a betting man, I'd wager that Overman spread some of his cash around."

Cain glanced down. "I wish I could refute that on principle, but human nature being what it is, I can't. Anything I can do to help in your crusade?"

"A copy of the Medical Examiner's report would be nice."

Cain shook his head. "You know I can't ask for that."

"This is a high-profile case. You haven't heard anything through the grapevine?"

Cain hesitated. "I guess since you're no longer the target of their investigation I can tell you this. I called a fishing buddy who works in the property department up there."

"Why did you do that?"

"Brannigan phoned me after they were down here under the pretense of getting more background on you and your business. He made it clear that you were guilty as far as he was concerned, and it made me curious. My friend said the girl had ten grams of coke and over two-hundred bucks in her purse." He handed him a folded piece of paper. "He e-mailed me an inventory of what they found at the crime scene."

Nick scanned the page. "Two-hundred-sixty isn't even spare change for Kristine."

"If she'd just made a buy, that would explain it."

"Yeah, it would." He thought for a minute. "Can you ask around unofficially and see what you can find out about J.P. Overman?"

"Why?"

"I'm trying to get a clear picture of what I'm up against."

Cain stood. "What you're up against is one very wealthy man who has put politicians in office and derailed the careers of anyone who crossed him. Now he's trying to prove you killed his daughter. Good luck."

Rock had printed off the photo Nick e-mailed and was about to show it to his staff. He was in one of the casinos when he was paged to come to the bar.

"You have a phone call, Rock," the woman working behind the bar said.

Rock picked up the phone. "This is Bianco."

"Bianco, this is J.P. Overman."

"What the hell do you want?"

"I have a proposition for you," Overman replied with his typical bluster.

"If you're lookin' to buy in, forget it. I don't need a partner."

"I'm not interested in your business. I'm prepared to offer you five-hundred-thousand dollars, tax free, in an offshore account."

Rock paused. "In exchange for what?"

"One phone call to the Broward County prosecutor. Call McCorkle and tell him you have proof that Nick Seven killed my daughter, and the money's yours. No questions asked."

Rock laughed. "Ya know, Overman, I always heard you weren't playin' with a full deck. This just confirms it. I wouldn't perjure myself to a D.A., especially for you. What happens when he asks me for this so-called proof?"

"I'll take care of that. You won't be at risk for exposure."

"Forget it."

"Don't be too hasty, Bianco. This offer is better than the alternative."

"What alternative?"

"Who do you think put the director of the Florida gaming commission in office? The same with the chairman of the alcoholic beverage control board. One call from me and you could find yourself the subject of scrutiny. Do me this service, and you can avoid the spotlight."

"No sale."

"Bianco, I know a great deal about you, including your ties with certain parties that the justice department is interested in. Even the hint of an investigation could get your gaming license suspended."

"If you know anything about my friends, you know how they feel about people who snitch to the Feds and how they handle it. Go screw yourself."

He slammed the phone down. *Amateur.*

CHAPTER TEN

The afternoon sun had passed from one side of Key Largo to the other, traversing from ocean to Gulf, preparing for the final phase of its daily journey. A light breeze blew in, rustling the palm fronds and banyan trees that outlined the perimeter of the deck outside Nick's condo. Calypso music from one of the restaurants further down the channel drifted in, accompanied by the sounds of laughter and chatter.

Nick lay on a chaise, staring at the vista through sunglasses. He adjusted his position in an attempt to get comfortable and felt a twinge of pain when he turned the wrong way. He gently rubbed his right side, the one that had taken the hardest impact from the assault he had received the night before. *When I catch up with that son of a bitch Junior, we'll have a conversation that's light on words and heavy on actions. I never did like him.*

He used his time to reflect on everything that had happened so far. This was part of his trouble. Whenever Nick had a puzzle to solve and a piece didn't want to fit where he placed it, he obsessively worked it over and over in his mind until he found where it belonged. Then he went to work on the next piece. It had made him a good field agent, but a lousy civilian. The current ill-fitting piece was tied to one word — why? A simple little word, used in everyday discourse, but applied to many things.

Why is Overman intent on proving that I killed Kristine? I know we didn't get along, but I wrote it off as good old-fashioned snobbery, one of the privileged looking down his nose at the rest of us.

He found himself wondering how the Fort Lauderdale cops had gotten his service record, which was supposed to be locked up in a government warehouse, but attributed it to the work of Overman's money. *I spent enough time around the Beltway to know how these things work. You handpick your candidate, secretly finance their campaign, stock the rallies with people hoisting signs for a few bucks, and make sure they show up at the polls on election day with a sawbuck in their pocket and the candidate's name on a slip of paper. When you need a favor, you call The Chosen One, and your wish is granted. A very tidy way to run an empire.*

Nick was brought out of his daydream by his ringing cell phone.

"This is Rock. I showed that picture to my floorwalkers and we got a hit. One of my guys recognized him."

"He's a regular?"

"Every night. Comes out at eight, gone by eleven."

"What made him stand out?"

"Erratic betting habits. My man said this guy hangs around the roulette and crap tables, never bets more than a few bucks, then drifts in and out of the room."

"Your floorwalker has good eyes."

"That's what they're paid for."

"I'm coming up there this evening. If this guy shows, I want to talk to him."

"You think he killed the Overman kid?"

"I think he had some connection with her. I want to find out what it was."

He disconnected as Felicia joined him and sat at the table.

"Feel like taking a trip to the Gold Flamingo tonight?" he asked.

"What we goin' out there for?"

"Some answers. The man in that pic you made is a regular customer."

"Why don't you just tell the cops so they can pick him up?"

"Because he can invoke his right to have an attorney

present. I want to ask him some questions in my own way."

"You sure you feel up to it?"

"Oh yeah."

"Nick, I've been thinkin' about why this rich guy's gunnin' for you."

"I'm listening."

"You suppose he's connected with the CIA?"

Nick thought for a few moments. "Could be. I'm sure Overman knows important people in D.C. Hell, he probably sent half the Florida legislators there. Are you thinking that someone got to him because of something I did when I was on active duty?"

She shrugged. "It's just a thought. You know how many people you pissed off who might still be holdin' a grudge."

He nodded. "No argument, but try this one. Overman's company has a lot of foreign business interests, not all of them reputable. What if one of them wanted to use his connections in Washington and he refused?"

"You think someone killed his daughter to get his cooperation?"

"A job like that would be tailor-made for the types of covert organizations we used to deal with. Take her out of the picture, then find a fall guy to pin it on, like a former boyfriend she just had a public fight with."

"What does his company do?"

"Commercial real estate, corporate mergers, and venture capital management, among other things. Basically, anything that'll fatten his wallet." He paused as something came back to him. "A few years ago, there was a big protest outside his office that got pretty ugly. Overman leveraged the buyout of a local manufacturer then sent all the jobs to Argentina. Put more than a thousand people out of work."

"That would piss off a lot of folks. You think that has some connection to his kid gettin' killed?"

"It's another angle to explore."

Dusk descended over the coast, turning the sky from daylight blue to nighttime azure mixed with splashes of orange. Nick and Felicia stood at the railing of a water taxi, a cooling breeze ruffling their hair. Nick shifted his left arm to get comfortable with the Walther PPK in his shoulder holster. When they docked at The Gold Flamingo, they went to Rock's office.

He looked Nick up and down. "How does the other guy look?"

"When I catch up with him, I'll let you know."

"What's your game plan?"

"Hang around the casino until our man shows up then follow him. I may need some help."

"Way ahead of you. One of my guys will shadow you and back your play." He smiled at Felicia. "My apologies for ignoring you, Ms. Hagens. How are you this evening?"

Felicia returned his smile. "Fine, thank you."

"Does this guy always hang out in the room where I saw him the other night?" Nick asked.

"Yeah."

Nick glanced at his watch. "It's show time."

He and Felicia ascended to the casino on the second floor, which was already crowded. They stopped at the cashier's cage, and Nick purchased two-hundred dollars' worth of tokens. He gave half to Felicia.

"What you need me to do?" she asked.

"Mingle and keep your eyes open. If you see the guy we're looking for, text me."

They separated and went to different parts of the room. Nick stopped at one of the roulette tables, placed a bet then casually glanced at the other players, not finding his subject.

"Twenty-three red," the croupier announced when the wheel came to a stop. He paused a moment then addressed

Nick. "Hey, buddy, I said twenty-three red."

Nick looked at him. "Huh?"

He pointed at the table. "You won."

Nick scooped up his winnings. "Thanks."

He pocketed the chips and went to the bar. Across the room, Felicia casually roamed among the gamblers, stopping to drop some tokens into a slot machine. Nick ordered a scotch and soda, then took a small sip while scanning the faces. His cell phone buzzed and he read the text Felicia had sent him.

"Crap table, center of room."

Nick set his drink on the bar and went in that direction. He glanced over his shoulder and saw one of the floorwalkers, a burly bald-headed man of Brazilian descent wearing a black tux, following at a leisurely pace. Nick's focus narrowed when he saw the object of his search standing at the table, making sloppy bets by setting chips on the table then not paying attention to the dice action. After a few minutes he looked at his watch, then went toward the exit.

Nick, Felicia and the floorwalker followed at a safe distance. They watched the man take the steps to the observation deck but waited a few minutes before following him. When they reached the top, Nick stopped and held up his hand. He heard a man and woman's voice, talking in low tones. He looked at Felicia and signaled for her to go to the far side of the bulkhead in the middle of the deck.

Nick gave her a few minutes then quietly emerged on the deck with the floorwalker close by. They stopped and listened.

"Geez, I don't know, Eddie," the young woman said. "Five-hundred's a lot of money."

"Hey, this stuff would run you twice that in South Beach," he replied. "But I guess if you don't want it . . ."

"No, I'll take it," she quickly replied. "I need it."

Nick peered around the bulkhead and saw her exchange cash for a small baggie of white powder. He drew his gun from his shoulder holster, then stepped into sight.

"Hands in the air," he barked.

The woman tried to run away but the floorwalker grabbed her arm. The man made a quick retreat in the opposite direction around the bulkhead. A moment later Nick heard him cry out in pain. Felicia emerged escorting the man with one of his arms pinned behind his back. His other hand held a handkerchief to his bleeding nose.

"You broke my nose, you bitch!" he exclaimed.

"What a shame," Felicia responded.

She marched him to Nick but maintained her firm grip. Nick searched the man's pockets then held up four more baggies, two with smaller pouches containing white powder and the other two containing capsules.

"My, my, what have we here?" he asked while examining them. "Looks like major weight."

The man took deep breaths while holding his nose. "You a cop?"

"Worse. I'm the guy you set up as Kristine Overman's killer and I'm pretty pissed about it, so choose your words carefully."

Rock and another bouncer emerged from the stairwell.

"What the hell is this?" he demanded.

Nick held up the drugs. "Someone's running a side business on your boat."

Rock took a few steps forward with his fist doubled up and his face contorted in anger.

Nick held up his hand. "First things first." He addressed the young woman. "You know this guy?"

She rapidly nodded. "His name's Eddie Parks. He's my . . ." She stopped short and cast her gaze down.

"Connection?" Nick finished.

She nodded again.

Rock stuck his finger in her face. "Get the hell off my boat and don't ever come back," he growled.

"What about my money?"

"Quit while you're ahead."

Nick held his gun straight up, jacked the slide on top to force a bullet into the chamber, then lowered it to waist level. He took slow steps toward Parks and locked onto his eyes while keeping his gun in place.

"The other night you were in the casino when I was. You followed Kristine when she left the room. A half-hour later, she's dead and the cops think I did it. Convince me that I shouldn't tear your arm off and beat you to death with it."

Parks shook his head. "You got it wrong. I saw the fight you two had and I followed her out of the casino, but I didn't kill her."

"Be more convincing."

He let out a deep breath while keeping his handkerchief pressed against his nose. "We were supposed to meet up here to . . . you know . . . do business, but she stopped me in the passageway and said she had something to take care of first. Told me to meet her up here later."

"I guess she found a cheaper dealer."

He gave a confused look. "What are you talkin' about?"

"She had two bags of coke in her purse when she went overboard. Looks like someone beat you to the score."

He shook his head. "She wasn't buying coke from me. She was selling it to me."

Nick's brow furrowed. *I didn't see that one coming.* "You're telling me that Kristine Overman was supplying your drugs?"

He hesitated. "She had a connection in South Beach. What she didn't use herself she sold to me. Always had the best stuff, pure gold."

"Which I'm sure you cut several times to make more profit. Was this a regular thing?"

"I think she did it just for kicks. She'd call me when she had a surplus and we'd arrange to meet."

"You do all your deals on my boat?" Rock asked.

Parks hesitated. "This is one of my regular stops so my customers know where to find me."

Nick processed his confession. "This other thing Kristine had to take care of. What was it?"

"I don't know. When I heard all the commotion and found out it was her that went overboard, I hauled ass back to shore."

Nick lowered his gun then looked at Rock. "Your call."

Rock addressed the two bouncers. "Show this guy that we don't want his kind out here, then take what's left of him to the mainland. Call the cops and tell 'em where they can pick up their garbage." He took the drugs from Nick then handed them over. "Make sure these are in his pockets." He addressed Nick. "Let's go to my cabin."

They took the stairs below decks to Rock's private lair. When they were seated, Rock poured a round of drinks then passed the glasses across the desk. He plopped into his chair, took a long swallow and lit a cigar.

"I can't believe this shit," he muttered. "I hire the best security team money can buy and they let this happen. Someone's ass is gonna be raw in the morning."

Nick sipped his drink. "Don't take it so hard, Rock. These things happen."

"You think that guy killed the Overman kid?"

"Parks doesn't have the stones to beat someone to death with his bare hands."

"I don't follow."

Nick took another sip then looked at Felicia. "I'm getting a headache. Would you explain it to him?"

She cleared her throat. "We watched the security tapes. Whoever killed that girl was revved up when he did it."

"You mean high?" Rock asked.

"No, more like totally pissed off. He was really into beatin' her up before he tossed her over. It looked very personal."

Rock shook his head. "That means there's still a killer out there."

"And J.P. Overman is convinced it's me," Nick finished.

Rock took a puff then chased it with whiskey. "Then I should tell you something. Overman called and offered me a half a million bucks if I'd tell the cops I had proof you did it."

"I'm glad we're friends. That's a lot of free money to pass up."

"His money I don't want. Too many strings attached."

"What did you tell him?"

"I told him to go screw himself." He looked at Felicia. "Excuse me, miss."

"I've heard worse," Felicia replied.

"You know, he could cause trouble for you," Nick commented. "Overman has a lot of friends."

"I have friends, too, and some of 'em owe me favors, if you get my drift."

Nick took a sip. "What do you really know about Overman?"

"The same things you do—he's an arrogant asshole who thinks with his bank account."

"What about the stuff you don't read in the media?"

Rock gave a gruff chuckle. "You mean does he have any dirt under his nails?"

"Yeah."

He rolled his cigar between his fingers. "I may know some people who can answer that."

CHAPTER ELEVEN

Somewhere in the morning fog of consciousness a telephone was ringing. Nick tried ignoring it, thinking he was dreaming, but it wouldn't cease its relentless racket. He reached for the phone on the nightstand and brought it to his ear under the covers.

"Yeah?" he mumbled.

"Nick, this is Ted Cain. Are you awake?"

Nick sat up and squinted at the clock. "You've got a helluva nerve, calling me before noon."

"I think you'll be glad I did. I just saw you as the lead story on one of the local morning talk shows."

Nick suddenly came awake. "What the hell are you talking about?"

"*A.M. Miami* just aired an interview with J.P. Overman about his daughter's murder. He said since the police hadn't made an arrest, he was taking matters into his own hands. He named you, and announced the wrongful death suit he filed."

Nick stood and slipped into a pair of shorts. "When was this on?"

"A few minutes ago. You can see it online."

Nick hurried downstairs, carrying the phone with him. He booted up his computer and typed in the website. He saw Overman's photo in one of the windows, under the banner "Justice Sought for Society Killing."

"Okay, I see it."

"Do me a favor. Before you watch it, take a few deep breaths and remember that you're no longer licensed to kill."

Nick groaned. "Give me some credit, will ya? I'll call you back."

Felicia padded into the room, rubbing sleep from her eyes. "What's all the ruckus?"

Nick clicked on the story. "Cain called to tell me I made the morning news."

Felicia came around the desk to watch with him. Nick's pulse sped up as he watched Overman name him as the obvious suspect in Kristine's killing. He also slammed the police and prosecutor for allowing this menace to society to remain at large.

"Can he get away with that?" Felicia asked.

"He just did."

The phone rang and Felicia answered it. "Who did you say this was?" she asked, then covered the mouthpiece to address Nick. "It's a reporter from the Miami Herald askin' for a comment on that story we just saw. You wanna talk to him?"

Nick took the phone from her. "Who is this?" He listened for a couple of moments. "No comment, and don't call again."

He disconnected then tossed the phone onto the desk. "Do you believe this shit?"

"I can't believe he can go on the air like that and say any damn thing he wants about you."

Nick grabbed the phone and punched in his lawyer's number. "Grand, this is Nick." He paused. "Yeah, I just watched it. What can we do about it?" Another pause followed. "All right. Thanks."

"Well?"

"Grand said he's filing an emergency motion for a gag order. He's arguing that any pre-trial publicity will taint the jury pool in that civil suit Overman filed."

"Jury?" Felicia exclaimed. "You think this is gonna go to trial?"

Nick put his hands on her arms and gazed into her eyes,

trying to downplay the situation. "Probably not, but this is how he has to approach it." He pulled her in for a hug. "Calm down, angel. We were only served with this crazy suit yesterday. These things take years. And besides, this isn't the worst problem we've ever faced."

"Doesn't mean I have to like it."

Nick ran his palm along her bare shoulder. "I don't like it, either."

Captain Kruger opened the door to his office and cast his gaze around the squad room.

"Brannigan and Cortez," he called out. "My office. Now!"

The Detectives entered his office and closed the door. They were about to sit when Kruger stopped them.

"You won't be here long enough to get comfortable," he said, his voice harsh with irritation. "Where are you on finding the guy in that picture Seven showed us, the one from the Gold Flamingo?"

"Nowhere," Cortez said. "We put out a BOLO, but he hasn't turned up yet."

Kruger picked up a photo from his desk and handed it over. "Your suspect is in the intensive care ward at Holy Cross Hospital. A patrol unit found him outside the Sailfish Marina last night after they received an anonymous call."

Brannigan's brow furrowed when he looked at the photo. "Looks like someone used him for a punching bag." He flipped through the accompanying document. "Broken nose, broken jaw, three broken ribs, slight concussion, and too many contusions to count. Did he say who did this to him?"

"He said he slipped on a wet floor when he was leaving Bianco's boat."

"He's covering for somebody."

"Wow, Phil," Kruger said. "Your grasp of the obvious is truly amazing. I can see why you're a detective."

Brannigan flashed him an icy look.

"Did they find anything else?" Cortez asked.

"Two bags of cocaine, two dozen fentanyl capsules and a boatload of cash in his pockets. His ID says he's Edward Parks, with an address in Liberty City. Run his name through narcotics. What else are you doing in the Overman girl's murder?"

"Drawing a blank," Cortez answered. "Her cell phone was too badly damaged for the lab to get anything usable from the memory card. We spoke with the people who were with her that night, but no one's saying anything useful."

"Probably afraid of pissing off her old man," Brannigan added.

Kruger let loose an exasperated breath. "You fellas have had all week to work on this, and you haven't come up with anything. Should I reassign this case to someone else?"

"Hold it, Cap," Brannigan said. "We had a perfectly good suspect but you and McCorkle told us to let him go."

"A suspect who made us look like idiots," Kruger said. "The next time you think you have someone viable, make damn sure you can back it up. This thing has drug trafficking written all over it. The victim had cocaine on her person, and we have someone else who was on the scene the night she was murdered, also involved in drugs. Do either of you see a possible connection here?"

The detectives looked at each other.

"Yes," Cortez said. "We'll concede that drugs may have played a factor in this."

"Outstanding," Kruger said in a curt voice. "Get with narcotics and work that angle. Chances are very good that you might actually come up with a suspect. And talk to this Parks guy, but do it right this time, because I'm not gonna eat another bucket of brownies."

Early evening was mild, after a light rain had drifted over the Keys that afternoon. The atmospheric change brought out more brilliant colors for the sunset. The sky over the Gulf was a pleasant palette of orange, yellow and blue, with a few left-over clouds adding contrast.

Nick and Felicia entered Cricket's. It had been a tense day after the rude awakening they had gotten that morning. Felicia had suggested that they skip work that night, but Nick knew they both needed to get out of the house and be around people. He became aware of customers giving him odd looks when they went to the bar, accompanied by murmuring in low voices. He motioned for Raul to come over.

"What's going on?" he asked.

Raul nervously cast his gaze from side to side before answering in a low voice. "Have you seen what's been posted on Twitter, chief?"

Nick shook his head. "I don't follow social media."

Raul took out his cell phone. "Maybe you should."

He tapped one of the apps then showed Nick and Felicia a post on J.P. Overman's page. It rehashed what he had said on TV that morning, but in more vitriolic terms. Nick's heart pounded when he read the words "serial killer" and "government-trained assassin turned loose on an unsuspecting public." The next post continued in the same vein, saying in explicit terms that Nick alone was responsible for killing Kristine.

That son of a bitch. "Is that why I'm getting all these funny looks?"

Raul nodded. "We had some cancellations for dinner reservations, too. Sorry, chief."

"He can't do this," Felicia asserted angrily.

"According to the first amendment, he can," Nick said.

"But he maligned you on a public forum," Felicia argued. "That's slander."

"Good luck proving it," Nick said. "I'll be outside."

Nick fixed a drink then went to his private table, ignoring the sideways glances he was getting. He tried to lose himself in the usually tranquil viewing of the sunset, but his internal rage was close to boiling.

Felicia joined him with her own drink. "I talked with one of the servers. Overman posted somethin' about you on Instagram, too."

"Like what?"

She hesitated. "Your picture, along with the address for the club. He said more of the same trash talk, too. That's prob'ly why some of our reservations bailed."

"I guess in times like these, you find out who your real friends are."

"Hon, there must be somethin' we can do."

Nick took a long swallow of scotch and soda, thinking. "Maybe there is."

"What're you thinkin'?"

He looked at her. "Two can play this game. Overman's a public figure with a nasty business reputation. There must be someone out there with an axe to grind who wouldn't mind sharing what they know about him."

"Where will you get what you need?"

"Do you remember Bill Ceretta, the guy who writes for one of the weekly papers down here?"

Felicia nodded. "I thought you didn't like talkin' to reporters."

"He's always treated me pretty good. Maybe he wouldn't mind being generous again."

Nick went to his office and rummaged through the business cards in his desk drawer until he found the one he needed. He picked up the phone and punched in the cell number from the card.

"Hey, Bill, it's Nick Seven from Cricket's. How are you?"

"That's not why you called," Ceretta replied in his slight New Jersey twang. "Any time you ask me how I am, the last thing you want to know is how am I. What's up?"

"Where you doing your off-duty drinking these days?"

"If you want to catch me tonight, I'm at Snapper's."

"Sit tight. I'll be there in fifteen."

He told Felicia where he was going then made the drive south to Tavernier. Snapper's on the Water was located on the Atlantic side of the island, in an old conch building sandwiched between an old marina and a newer resort. Nick found a parking space, then went inside. He found his party sitting alone on the outdoor deck overlooking the ocean.

A small band played off to the side, but the customers seemed oblivious to the local musicians vying for their attention and tips. Nick approached the table and eyed Ceretta. He was of average build, with gray-streaked hair pulled into a ponytail, offset by a Van Dyke beard. He had a martini in front of him, which he sipped sparingly. Nick pulled up a chair.

"Been awhile," Ceretta said. "I never get a call from you, unless you want something."

Nick chuckled. "I'll try not to be so transparent next time."

A waitress came by and took Nick's drink order. He waited until she returned with it before continuing his conversation.

"I need some information," he said.

"Would this have anything to do with your sudden emergence on social media?"

"That got around fast."

Ceretta shrugged. "It's a small island. What do you need?"

Nick took a drink. "What do you know about J.P. Overman?"

"You want the press release version or the truth?"

"The real deal."

"Funny thing about him. He's one of the most public fig-ures down here, aside from the celebrities who live on Star Island, but nobody knows much about him."

"Including you?"

Ceretta flashed a sly grin. "Nothing gets past these eyes. Overman's made a career out of manipulating the media for his own good, to make himself look better than he is. He uses that to hide a lot of secrets, but I know people who don't mind talking out of school. What are you looking for?"

"Did you see the shit he posted about me online?"

Ceretta chuckled. "Oh, yeah. A real hatchet job."

"I'm afraid he's just getting warmed up, and I want to cut him off."

"Give me a day or so. I might be able to help you out."

"You aren't worried that he may come after you?"

"Call me crazy, but once in a while I like to live danger-ously. Did you know that before the New York Times broke the Hollywood sex harassment scandal, two reporters turned it down because they were afraid of payback? How do you suppose they're feeling now?"

"Like they missed a great opportunity. Anything you can tell me to get started?"

"If you want to know what you're up against, check the online archives for the local TV stations. During a press con-ference last year, Overman didn't like a question one of the reporters asked him, and he went on this incoherent rant that had nothing to do with the subject. Two of his handlers prac-tically had to drag him out of the room. It was a major melt-down."

"Just to be clear, I don't want you getting in trouble over this."

Ceretta shrugged. "Consider it payback."

"For what?"

He glanced down for a few moments. "My old man and two of my brothers worked for an electronics manufacturer just north of Miami. My dad was a lifer, within a year of retirement. Overman's company leveraged a buyout and sent all the jobs overseas."

Nick sat back and crossed his arms over his chest. "Sorry to hear that. Did they bounce back?"

"My brothers got into something else, but my dad wasn't so lucky. About the only thing he could get was a janitorial job and some part-time work during harvest season at the citrus farms." Ceretta looked at him. "He keeled over from a heart attack last year. I'd like to see someone knock Overman down a few pegs."

CHAPTER TWELVE

Nick sat on the deck watching the late morning sun as it crested over Key Largo, while the palms swayed gently. The heat was on its way to the predicted high of 85, but a soothing breeze drifted in, bringing the scent of sea water from the nearby channel. A charter fishing boat departed from one of the marinas down the waterway, its diesel engines gurgling as it navigated the narrow inlet.

He sipped his coffee, then looked at Felicia, who was pacing near the railing with her arms crossed and her gaze cast downward. The events of the previous day had given her a restless night, and her nocturnal kicking had kept Nick awake, too.

She's really taking this hard. Wish I could do something to make things better, but my hands are tied. All I can do is wait, but what am I waiting for? The next shoe to drop? Receiving some info from Ceretta that I can use?

He looked at the screen on his phone that displayed Overman's daily missile strike, then set it face down on the table.

He's upping his game by including speculation about my late wife. Where the hell is he getting his info? He hasn't gone into too many details, but I closed that part of my life a long time ago. If I weren't so pissed about this, I could almost get a laugh out of him referring to me as a second-rate hitman. I just don't like his implication that I was involved in her death. That was never brought up at the time.

He stood and approached Felicia. He placed his hands on her upper arms and she looked up at him. He gave the most convincing impression of his laidback, cool smile he could come up with.

"This is a switch, you pacing," he said. "Usually I'm the one burning off nervous energy. Want to talk about it?"

She let out the deep breath she had been holding. "There's somethin' I'd like to know."

"What?"

She looked into his eyes. "How can you be so damn calm about this? Why am I the one doin' all the worryin'?"

"You aren't. I'm just trying not to let it show."

"You're doin' a damn good job of it."

Nick laughed. "Only what you can see from the outside. Inside, I'm fuming."

"Then why aren't you doin' somethin'?"

"Like what? You want me to go to Overman's house and challenge him to a duel? Maybe take him hostage and demand a retraction of all those nasty-grams he posted?"

Felicia laughed softly. "Okay, tough guy. You made your point."

Nick took her hands in his. "I think we both need to get out of here. How about I take you to lunch at your favorite place?"

"You must really think I need cheerin' up."

"Not only that, but we'll stop at that shop you like on the way back, the one that sells those Key Lime products."

"This is almost as good as that spa day you treated me to at the resort."

Marker 88 restaurant, on the southern tip of Islamorada, evoked the typical Florida Keys experience. The outdoor dining area was situated under a grove of palms providing natural shade and a tropical atmosphere. The indoor section was right out of the fine dining guide, with linen tablecloths and bone china. A dock near the outdoor area extended fifty feet into the Gulf, and a few boats were moored there, the passengers having come ashore to enjoy the local fare and fresh catch the restaurant was known for.

Nick and Felicia occupied one of the tables under the palms. During a lunch consisting of conch fritters and grilled mahi-mahi, they had avoided any talk of their current troubles. Whenever it seemed like the conversation was heading in that direction, Nick had changed course and talked about something else.

She sipped her iced tea. "This has been really nice. I always liked this place. Reminds me of home."

Nick sat back. "I think we should plan a trip to Barbados in the near future."

"Why?"

"Because that's the second time this week you've made a reference like that. You said the same thing the other night when we were dodging waves on the beach."

She glanced down and gave a shy smile while brushing back a strand of hair from her face. "Maybe I'm thinkin' of simpler times."

"Times when you weren't dodging bullets or looking over your shoulder?"

Felicia raised her gaze to meet his. "It's my defense mechanism. Don't you ever do that, think about times when your biggest worry was who you'd ask to the dance, or what you wanted for Christmas?"

He propped one leg on the other. "There are things I get nostalgic about, when my own life was a bit simpler. I stop and realize that I wasn't always this complex maze of mixed emotions and internal demons."

"When did those demons take up residence?"

Nick thought for a few moments. "After I was forced to go out on my own when my family was killed by a drunk driver when I was in high school. That shattered any illusions I may have had about a white picket fence life in suburbia."

"What's your favorite memory from before that?"

"I guess it would be the vacation trips we took every summer. My dad would take two weeks off, we'd load up the car and go someplace different each year. It was a great educational experience and made me want to see more of the world."

"Did you spend much time at the beach when you were a kid?"

Nick chuckled. "There weren't any of those around Dayton, Ohio. The only time I saw genuine beach sand was if we traveled to the Jersey Shore."

"Sounds like a typical Midwest upbringing."

"Just a textbook middle-class family."

"It must've been tough to lose them your senior year in high school."

Nick hesitated at the memory. "It was. I stayed with my mom's sister and her husband until I graduated, then I joined the Army. We were between wars so I used that time to get a bachelor's in pre-law, then joined the CIA when my hitch was up. You know the rest."

Felicia took another drink. "Nick, I appreciate you tryin' to keep me distracted, but you don't have to put on a brave face for me."

He gave a sheepish grin. "Guess I didn't pull that off very well, did I?"

"I saw what Overman posted today, and I know how much you hate thinkin' about that part of your life. It's okay for you to be angry. Hell, you can even break somethin' if you want."

"That's very generous of you, but I'm not that mad."

"The way I'm readin' this, we have two things to figure out — why did someone kill the girl, and why does Overman want to frame you for it?"

"The second one may be easier to answer. Perhaps he knows who did it and wants to cover it up. If it was due to his financial hide-and-seek, he may think he needs to divert suspicion so nothing embarrassing comes out."

"You think he'd let his daughter's killer get away with it to save his business?"

"I wouldn't put much past him. The guy's ruthless. To him, people are like tissues—when you're through using them, you toss them out."

"You said he runs his family like a dictatorship. Is he a control freak?"

Nick dredged a few things from his memory. "More like a cold fish. Aloof, distant, demanding, withholding affection." He laughed softly. "I never gave it much thought before this, but I remember he had an old portrait of Stalin hanging in his private study."

"Why would he have a dictator's portrait on display?"

"It's probably his role model. It certainly reflects the way he runs his business."

"I still can't figure why someone wanted to murder his kid."

"I think it was the drug angle. If Kristine was dealing like Parks said she was, she might've wandered onto someone's turf at some point. On a popular nightspot like Rock's boat, the message would come through loud and clear—don't screw with us."

Felicia shook her head. "I don't buy it. You saw how enraged the killer was on that video. It looked personal to me."

Nick thought. "That's a good point. She didn't try to run, and they were arguing before he killed her. It was someone she knew."

"Like a boyfriend?"

"Could be. I know Kristine used to get on my nerves, and according to her old man, I'm a human time bomb waiting to go off. I'm surprised I didn't kill her myself years ago."

Felicia laughed then squeezed his hand. "I'm glad you're keepin' your sense of humor through all this."

CHAPTER THIRTEEN

R aul cruised south on U.S. 1 the next morning in his old Camaro Z28. He sang along with the music on a Spanish radio station from Miami. The window was down and the morning breeze felt good. He glanced at the clock in the dash, then slowed as he neared a gas station/convenience store. He parked and went inside, not bothering to lock the car. Several minutes later he emerged with a cup of coffee and a pocketful of lottery tickets.

He continued his journey and checked the clock again, judging the time and how far he was from Cricket's. He yawned. *I need to talk to the chief about gettin' someone else to work these turnarounds. By the time we close and I drive all the way home to Florida City, it's after two in the morning. Days like this when I have to come back here to get the club open for lunch are cuttin' into my booty time.*

He heard the short burst of a police siren and looked in the rearview mirror. A Monroe County sheriff's car was directly behind him with lights flashing. Raul pulled over to the side of the road and shut off the engine. He watched in the side mirror as a deputy got out of the car and approached.

"Good morning," the officer said. "May I see your license and registration?"

Raul took the items from his wallet and handed them to the officer. He made notes on his ticket pad. "Would you step out of the vehicle, please?"

He unbuckled his seatbelt and did as requested. The deputy stepped back then indicated the rear of the car. "Stand over there."

Raul stood where indicated but was confused as he watched the deputy search the interior of the car. *I wasn't speedin', and my plates aren't expired. Why did he pull me over?*

The deputy stood upright, approached Raul and took his handcuffs from his belt. "Sir, you're under arrest. Turn around and place your hands behind your back."

Raul's eyes widened. "Arrest? For what?"

"Drug possession."

The ringing telephone brought Nick in from the deck outside his home, coffee cup in hand. He answered and was greeted by Rikita, his kitchen manager.

"Sorry to bother you at home, Nick, but Raul hasn't shown up yet. Can you come over and get the registers open?"

Nick's brow furrowed as he looked at the clock. *It's 10:30 and we open at eleven. Did he oversleep?*

"Did you try calling him?"

"Yeah, but no answer. We've got everything else ready to go."

"I'll be right over."

Felicia walked into the room. "What's up?"

"That was Rikita. She said Raul was a no-show this morning." He swallowed the last of his coffee. "I have to go over and get out the cash for the registers."

"I'll come with you."

They made the trip to Cricket's and had everything ready to open on time. Felicia ensured that the bar was prepped for the lunch crowd while Nick went outside and called Raul's cell. It went straight to voicemail. He went back inside and Felicia called him over to the bar. She held out the phone.

"Ted Cain for you."

Nick took the phone. "Yeah, Ted."

"Nick, can you come down to the lock-up on Stock Island?"

"Why?"

There was a short pause. "To visit Raul. He was arrested this morning on his way to work."

"On what charge?"

"Drug possession. Get here quick as you can."

He hung up, confused. *Raul with drugs? No way.*

"What's wrong, hon?" Felicia asked.

"Raul was busted for drug possession this morning. That's why he didn't show up."

"You're kiddin'," she said. "He doesn't do drugs."

Nick looked at her. "No, he doesn't. I'm going over to the jail to sort things out."

Stock Island, just north of Key West, originally boasted cattle that were raised there to satisfy carnivores who were tired of fresh catch. The County Sheriff's office and the jail now shared island space with the Key West Resort Golf Course and Tennessee Williams Fine Arts Center on one side, and several trailer parks on the other that even the police tended to avoid after dark.

Nick parked in the visitor's lot, dropped his sunglasses into the console and went inside. A few minutes later he was joined by Ted Cain, who escorted him into the holding cell area.

"What can you tell me?" Nick asked while they walked.

"Patrol pulled him over this morning just north of Tarpon Basin Drive," Cain replied. "They tossed the car and found a stash of marijuana."

"Why did they pull him over? Was he speeding or driving erratically?"

Cain hesitated. "Dispatch received an anonymous call that a car matching his belonged to a dealer, and they were on their way to make a delivery."

Nick stopped and looked at him. "An anonymous call? You've gotta be kidding me."

"It's procedure, Nick. You know that. When someone reports suspected drug activity, we have to check it out."

"Ted, there's no way that grass belonged to Raul. He has a clean record and he doesn't do drugs."

Cain poked his finger in Nick's chest. "Before you go all defense attorney on me, hear me out. I know it's probably a set-up, so I asked the lab to dust the package for fingerprints. If Raul's prints aren't on it, I'll make sure the prosecutor knows it."

They resumed their walk.

"Did he say anything?" Nick asked.

"Just that it didn't belong to him, and he doesn't know how it got into his car."

"Where in the car did your deputy find it?"

"Under the passenger seat. That's another reason I think it's a frame. If you're hauling drugs, you'd put them in the trunk, out of sight. The anonymous caller also provided Raul's license plate number."

They reached the visitation room and Ted unlocked the door to let Nick in.

"You can have five minutes," he said.

Nick paced the room but stopped when the door to the holding cell area opened. Raul came in, with a look on his face that was equal parts worry and confusion. They sat at the table.

"How you doing, amigo?" Nick asked in the calmest voice he could muster.

"I feel like I'm in a bad dream I can't wake up from." He looked into Nick's eyes. "Chief, you know I'm not dealin'."

"I know that. Tell me what happened before you were pulled over."

Raul took a deep breath. "I was on my way to work. I

stopped at a Gas 'n Go just north of Tradewinds Plaza. When I left, the cops pulled me over."

"What time was this?"

"About eight-thirty. I stopped there to get coffee and lottery tickets."

"Did you lock your car?"

He shook his head. "I was only gonna be gone a few minutes."

"Did you notice anyone hanging around when you went in?"

"No."

"What about at home? Did you see anyone around your apartment building that didn't belong?"

"Not that I remember. What the hell am I gonna do? They told me I could have a lawyer, but I don't know one."

"Don't worry about that. I'm calling my attorney to represent you."

"Is he any good?"

"Grand could find a loophole in the ten commandments. Do you need anything else?"

"I'll be all right."

Nick stood. "Hang in there."

Raul was taken back to his cell. When he was out of the room, Ted unlocked the door to the hallway and Nick joined him.

"How much grass did you find in Raul's car?" Nick asked.

"A hundred-and-eighty grams. Just to refresh your memory, anything over two-hundred grams is felony weight. What do you think happened?"

"I think whoever did this followed him from Florida City, waited until he pulled into that mini-mart then stashed the drugs while he was inside. Can you check the security cameras for that store?"

"I already sent one of my investigators over there. Who

would want to frame Raul as a drug mule?"

Nick stopped and looked into his eyes. "Only one name comes to mind—J.P. Overman."

"Why would Overman go after Raul?"

"To get to me. Let me know if you find anything at that store."

CHAPTER FOURTEEN

The northbound traffic on the Overseas Highway was moderate, but the numerous towns with reduced speeds Nick had to pass through on the drive from Stock Island made it a tedious trip. After spending nearly an hour as part of a long parade of RVs and cars hauling trailered boats, his patience was wearing thin. The scenery may have been calming and pleasant to look at, but he was oblivious to it at this point. His mind was preoccupied with the most recent salvo fired by his new arch enemy.

The son of a bitch is getting desperate. First he brings up my wife's murder, now he's going after my friends. What's next?

He pulled into his parking space outside Cricket's, and was glad to see a nearly full lot and exterior deck. Felicia greeted him when he walked inside.

"How is he?" she asked.

"He's hanging tough."

"Tell me what happened."

"An anonymous tipster said Raul was hauling drugs, and he got pulled over. They found marijuana under the passenger seat. Ted's convinced it's a set-up, and he's working it from that angle."

"You really think Overman was behind this?"

"I can't think of anyone else who'd want to make Raul look like a drug courier, and it's a classic move for someone like him. He can't break me down, so he goes after people close to me."

"How does this make you look guilty of killin' his

daughter?"

"It casts a bad light on my character and backs up all that crap he's been posting about me online. He's been calling me a hood, and painting me as a guy who associates with other criminal types. This makes it look valid."

Felicia shook her head. "I don't see how this helps him make a case against you."

"Ten to one he posts something on his damn Twitter page that I'm running drugs out of this place, and Raul was one of my dealers. He already implied to the cops that the cocaine in Kristine's purse was supplied by me."

"Are you gonna ask Grand to represent Raul?"

Nick nodded. "I called him from the jail. One of his associates is handling the arraignment. I just hope Ted gets the results of the fingerprint test back before then, so they can prove he didn't handle the package."

Two hours later, Nick stood at the inside bar, talking with one of the regulars, a crusty old charter fisherman named Happy Jack O'Halloran. He was the poster-boy for a deep-sea mariner, with his sun-beaten weathered face and rugged look, accented by several days' growth of gray beard and scraggly hair. He tossed back his straight shot of Irish whiskey and shuddered.

"You stockin' that cheap shit again, Seven?" he growled. "This stuff'll grow hair on oysters."

Nick chuckled. "Keep talking like that, and I'll make you pay your bar tab, Jack."

O'Halloran scoffed. "Fat chance. You need people like me to add a toucha class to this place. Gives the tourists the real Keys experience."

"In case you hadn't noticed, I run one of the high-end places. If you want to add ambience with your smelly clothes and fishing tales, go hang out at the Caribbean Club."

O'Halloran shook his head. "Can't do that. They banned

me."

"Get outta here. Why?"

O'Halloran leaned in close and lowered his voice. "Seems I created a stink in there one night when I mistook the interest of a pretty young lass who was passin' through. She didn't bother to mention that she had a fella with her when she started chattin' me up, so I made an exploratory move which he didn't appreciate. The management asked me to take my business elsewhere for a while."

Nick laughed. "Only you could get kicked out of a fisherman's bar."

His attention was diverted by a gray limo pulling up to the front entrance. The rear door opened and Raul got out, followed by Grand Logan. The car moved to a nearby parking space as they came inside.

Nick greeted Grand with a handshake then put his arm around Raul's shoulder. Felicia hurried from the other end of the bar and gave Raul a bear hug.

"You okay?" she asked.

"Yeah, I'm good," Raul said.

"Did anyone hurt you in jail?" Felicia asked. "If they did, I'll kick their ass."

He laughed. "No, I'm okay, but thanks."

"You want to take the rest of the day off?" Nick asked.

"I'd rather stay here and work, Chief. It'll get my mind off things."

Nick nodded. "Whatever you want." He addressed Grand. "I thought one of your junior partners was doing the arraignment."

"My schedule was light this afternoon so I decided to get out of the office," Grand replied. "I wanted to speak with you about your current problem and when the two appeared to be connected, I thought I should get directly involved."

He looked at Felicia and offered a warm smile. "How are

you, Felicia?"

She returned his smile. "Doing well, thank you. It's always nice to see you."

"Why don't we continue this outside?" Nick suggested.

He flagged down one of the servers to place an order, then they proceeded to Nick's table. The opened umbrella provided adequate shade from the mid-afternoon sun blazing in the clear blue sky. The server arrived a few minutes later with drinks and an assortment of appetizers on a platter.

"How did the arraignment go?" Nick asked.

"We got bail," Grand said. "The judge agreed to twenty-thousand since it was a first offense, cash or bond. I already posted it."

Nick's eyebrows arched. "That was very generous of you. I'll see that you get it back."

"Yes, you will," Grand said with a twinkle in his eye. "Actually, I'm not worried about it. I think this whole thing is a badly constructed frame." He sipped his scotch. "Tell me about this sheriff of yours, this Cain fellow. Trustworthy?"

"Yeah, he's a straight arrow, not like a lot of the small-town constables you hear about. He doesn't put people away just to make himself look good to the voters."

"You're on friendly terms?"

"I've known him since I first moved here. We go fishing, and he and his wife are regulars. What was your take?"

"About the same. In fact, he's one of the reasons we got low bail. He spoke up on Raul's behalf, something I don't often see from a police official."

"What did he say?"

"He pointed out that his lab didn't find Raul's fingerprints on the drugs, and vouched for his character."

Nick slowly nodded. "Glad to hear it. What did you want to see me about?"

"I've been reviewing our strategy for dealing with

Overman. I was going to request a gag order to put an end to his online harassment, but I'm not sure that's the way to go."

"But he's defamin' Nick in public with a lot of bullshit," Felicia said. "That isn't right."

"It may be uncomfortable to read, but it is his right to say what he wants," Grand replied. "Here's the bottom line—he's claiming everything he posts is factual. For Nick to refute it, he'd have to prove that it isn't. That means he'd be forced to tell his life story at some point." He looked at Nick. "Knowing what I know about your previous career, do you really want to take that chance?"

Nick took a fried shrimp from the plate, dunked it in hot sauce, then munched it while thinking. *He has a point. There are a lot of things in my file that wouldn't qualify as classified government secrets or national security. There are a lot of personal details, too.* "Not really."

"But hon," Felicia heatedly interjected, "he's callin' you a murderer and a crook. You can't let him get away with that."

"Felicia does have a point," Grand said. "Overman could technically be guilty of slander and defamation, if we can prove that his statements have caused you harm, or hurt your business."

"That's pretty tough to prove, isn't it?" Nick asked.

Grand nodded slowly. "Difficult, but not impossible. If we were to take him on, the one thing we could attack is his assertion that you were responsible for his daughter's death. Since you've already proved your innocence, we might have a shot with that."

"Speaking of which, I don't think that's going away anytime soon," Nick said. "Rock Bianco told me Overman offered him half-a-mil to tell McCorkle that I killed Kristine. He even offered to provide proof."

Grand laughed. "The man's arrogance knows no boundaries. That smacks of desperation. Do you really think he was behind that bogus drug bust this morning?"

"Absolutely. Raul isn't a drug dealer, and Cain said the whole thing was triggered by an anonymous call. Overman is the only person who'd benefit from a smear like that, something else he can use to make me look bad."

"Is Cain pursuing that angle?"

"He said one of his people was going to check the security video from the store Raul stopped at, so hopefully it captured whoever did this."

Grand finished his drink. "I feel like telling you to ride this out, but I'd probably be wasting my time. Just a word of caution, though—if you decide to climb into the mud pit with Overman, be sure that whatever you hit him with is irrefutable."

After Grand left, Nick and Felicia sat for a few moments.

"What are you gonna do?" she asked.

Nick looked at her. "Take up mud wrestling."

Rock Bianco stood at the bar in one of the casinos, reviewing the evening's agenda with his head of security, a tall, muscled man named Hackman. Rock's attention was diverted by the young Latina woman working behind the bar, who cleared her throat then nodded her head toward two men approaching.

Rock turned in that direction and his gaze narrowed when it came to rest on Brannigan and Cortez. His stomach growled as he wondered what fresh hell this was.

"Excuse the interruption," Brannigan said, "but we were in the neighborhood."

"One more reason for me to insist on reservations," Rock said. "What the hell is it this time?"

"Just a few questions about a customer who had an accident out here," Cortez said. "A guy named Edward Parks said he suffered a fall."

Rock smirked. "You guys get demoted to the ambulance chasing squad? Since when do the cops care about someone who was drunk and stumbled on the taxi dock?"

"When that someone winds up in ICU with injuries inconsistent with a fall," Cortez answered. "Want to tell us about it?"

Rock addressed Hackman. "Get me the paperwork on that guy who slipped the other night." He looked at the detectives. "It'll be a few minutes. You can amuse yourselves at the slots while you're waitin'."

Brannigan gave him a sharp look. "Keep it up, Bianco. Only a matter of time before I get something to hang on you."

"Dream on."

Hackman returned with a file folder and handed it to Rock. He removed a sheet of paper then gave it to Cortez.

"An accident report?" he asked.

"My insurance guy has us fill those out when someone is the victim of an unfortunate occurrence. Surprised you didn't know that anyone who owns a business has to do that."

"Pretty convenient," Cortez said.

"It's also the law. As you can see, Mr. Parks slipped on a wet spot on the passenger loading area when he was leaving for the evening."

"You said he was drunk. I don't see that listed anywhere."

"He refused medical treatment, which would've included a sobriety test. Guess he didn't want anyone to know how wasted he was."

"I see that he signed a waiver absolving you of any responsibility. Is that also standard procedure?"

Rock shrugged. "Happens all the time. People have a few too many, but decide not to file a claim."

"You ever settle for cash to keep your insurance premiums down?" Brannigan asked.

"It's been known to happen."

"We visited Parks in the hospital," Cortez said. "There's no way he got those injuries from slipping on a wet floor. He said two men took him to shore after his so-called accident. Were they your people?"

"When we saw that he was in distress, we offered to escort him to the mainland. It was the responsible thing to do."

"How do you explain the condition he was in when the patrol found him?"

"Perhaps he ran into someone he owed money to. Have you checked for any muggers working the docks?"

"Nice try," Brannigan said. "Parks claims a couple of your goons beat the hell out of him on your orders. In fact, he's thinking of pressing charges. You up for an assault complaint, Bianco?"

"He signed a waiver," Rock said. "That lets me off the hook."

"That isn't all he told us," Cortez said. "He said you knew he was selling drugs out here, and Kristine Overman was one of his customers. He said you knew that, too. Still want us to believe you don't know anything about her murder?"

Rock stared at him for a few moments. "I told you where I was when that went down, and I have witnesses."

"Just because you weren't there doesn't mean you didn't arrange it," Cortez said. "That's how contract killers work with guys like you, isn't it? We call that a conspiracy."

"I call it bluffing. Anything else?"

"Just that this is an ongoing investigation, until we learn who killed Overman and why," Cortez said. "If you'd like to make a statement, now would be a good time."

Rock gave him an intense stare. "Here's my statement— fuck off. Want me to put it in writing?"

"Might pay you to cooperate with us, Bianco," Brannigan said. "If you're connected to the murder, we'll find out."

"Knock yourself out," Rock said. "Now get the hell outta

here. I'm busy."

"We'll need a copy of that accident report," Cortez said.

Rock took his wallet from his pocket, fished out a business card and handed it over. "That's my attorney's number. Talk to him."

He watched Brannigan and Cortez leave the casino. "Damn cops," he muttered.

CHAPTER FIFTEEN

Evening in the Upper Keys was peaceful, with a cooling breeze and an ever-changing canvas of sunset. The area surrounding Nick's condo on the channel carried the distant sounds of people enjoying the tropical serenity and legendary Keys nightlife. Music with a rockabilly beat drifted in from Sharkey's Pub down the way, accompanied by the appetizing aroma of grilled steaks and fish from the Holiday Inn's poolside grill.

Nick sat in a chair on the deck, a glass of chardonnay on the table and his gaze taking in the calm horizon. Felicia sat next to him, cradling her glass in her lap.

"Sure is quiet out here tonight," she commented. "Just what we needed after today."

"Uh-huh," he absently answered.

She took a sip of wine. "You think Raul will come out of this thing okay?"

"Uh-huh."

She paused for a few moments. "Did you know that your hair turned pink and your pants are on fire?"

"Uh-huh." He looked at her. "Say what?"

"Just wanted to get your attention. You been in the twilight zone all evenin'. What's goin' on with you?"

He lay his head back, closed his eyes and laughed softly. "I was just thinking of something. When I quit the CIA and decided to settle here, I had this wild idea that all the drama in my life was in the past. What an idiot I was."

"Why you say that?"

"It seems like there's always something popping up to make me think I never really got out. It's like these recurring bad dreams I used to have."

"What happened in these dreams?"

"I'd be doing something routine, something I did every day, but I could never finish whatever it was. In another one, I'd be someplace familiar and try to leave, but something kept stopping me. I'd head for the exit, say in a parking lot or building, but I kept running into detours and roadblocks." He looked at her. "Do you think I'm crazy?"

"Because you had dreams that didn't make sense? If that qualifies you as crazy, you're in good company."

"You've had them, too?"

"Of course. Everybody has."

"What happens in yours?"

Felicia hesitated. "I don't think I should say."

"I told you mine. Yours can't be any crazier."

She looked into her glass as a smile spread across her face. "Okay, but don't laugh. When I was a teenager, I used to dream that I was walkin' alone on the beach. It was a clear day, the breeze was blowin', and the waves were washin' up on shore. I looked out to sea and I saw this guy swimmin' toward land. When he got closer, he walked out and stood there in baggie trunks and no shirt, lookin' at me."

She was silent.

"Well?" Nick asked. "Who was it?"

Felicia looked at him. "Tom Selleck, when he was on that TV show in Hawaii."

Nick burst into laughter. "You're kidding! You used to dream about running into Magnum on the beach?"

Felicia reached over and playfully smacked his arm. "I told you not to laugh. That show was on every day and I used to watch it."

His laughter died off. "Actually, that's very insightful."

"How so?"

"I didn't know you had a crush on a young Tom Selleck. Now I know what I'm competing against when we go to bed."

Felicia scooted her chair closer, set her glass on the table, then pulled Nick in for a lingering kiss.

"You're not competin' against anyone, tough guy. That was a teenager's crush. Didn't you crush on someone from TV or the movies when you were that age?"

Nick thought for a moment. "Yeah, I guess I did."

"Who?"

"Promise not to laugh?"

"Sure, just like you promised not to laugh at mine."

He waited a few moments. "Diana Rigg, from *The Avengers* TV show. I loved that black jumpsuit she wore."

Felicia giggled. "That's what I'd call insightful."

"How so?"

Felicia ran her fingers through his hair. "Because she was sexy in a kick-ass sort of way. Is that the kind of women you were attracted to?"

Nick kissed her. "Maybe when I was younger."

"What about now?"

He ran his palm along her cheek and peered into her eyes. "You tough kick-ass women still hold a certain appeal."

"I'm glad."

She placed her arms around his shoulders, moved closer and gave him a deep, tongue-probing kiss. Nick returned her fire and ran his hands along her shoulders. Her softness was a welcome treat after the tumultuous day they'd had, and he reveled in the closeness.

Their making out was interrupted by the sound of the doorbell from inside. Felicia pulled back slightly. "Someone's here."

"Ignore it. Maybe they'll go away."

He kissed her again, with more passion. He stopped in

mid-kiss when he heard a voice coming from the gate at the other end of the deck, where the walkway connected to the parking lot.

"Nick, are you home?"

They separated and Nick sighed when he recognized Ted Cain's voice.

"Come on in," he said.

Cain opened the gate then joined them. He stopped short when he saw their cuddle position and glasses of wine on the table. "Sorry. Guess I should've called first."

Felicia scooted her chair back while Nick sat up straight. "That's all right," he said. "Would you like a drink?"

"No, thanks. Mind if I sit down?"

Nick gestured at an empty chair. "What's up?"

Cain removed some photos from the folder he'd brought with him. "These are from the security camera at the store where Raul stopped this morning."

Nick looked at a photo of a husky Caucasian man roughly six feet tall, wearing a tropical-print shirt with tan trousers, his head lowered. The other shots showed him looking around the area then placing a package in Raul's car.

"Do you have any that show his face?"

Cain shook his head. "This guy was smart enough to keep his head down around the cameras." He handed over another photo. "But he wasn't so careful when he parked his car. We ran his license plate number. His name is Willie DeGarmo and he was let go from the Miami PD five years ago."

"What's he been doing since then?"

Cain paused. "Working as part of J.P. Overman's private security team, for twice what he was making as a cop."

Felicia let out a low whistle. "That's no coincidence."

"Sure isn't," Nick concurred. "Does this give you enough to pick him up?"

"Yeah. He wasn't very careful when he handled the

package, either. We requested his prints from the Miami police and they're a match for the ones we lifted from the bundle. We're bringing him in for questioning tomorrow. Looks like I owe you an apology."

"For what?"

"When you told me your conspiracy theory this morning, I had my doubts."

Nick shrugged. "No problem. I have trouble believing some of my theories, too. I want to thank you for what you did at the arraignment this afternoon. Speaking up for Raul was a classy thing to do, and I appreciate it."

Cain appeared to be embarrassed. "Just doing my job. That attorney of yours seems like a real piece of work, though."

"How so?"

"I got the impression that not much gets past him. Is he representing you in the Overman thing?"

"Yeah. He handled the meeting where I proved my innocence, and he's working on that damned civil suit, too."

Can settled back in his chair and propped one leg on the other. "Those online attacks seem to be getting more than a bit personal."

Nick looked at him. "Noticed that, did you?"

"Hard not to, since I know your history. Where's he getting his info?"

Nick drank some wine. "Probably from one of the political hacks he sent to Washington."

"I haven't forgotten that you asked me to poke into Overman's background. There isn't a whole lot there, except for what his press agent releases to the media."

"You're the second person who's told me that. How does a guy like him rise to public prominence without anyone knowing anything about his past?"

"One word — money."

Nick smirked. "Yeah, that old stuff. If you've got enough

of it, you can buy anyone's silence. I'll bet his lawyers work overtime writing non-disclosure agreements and paying hush money."

Cain gathered the photos then stood up. "I'll be on my way. Sorry to interrupt your evening but I thought you'd want to see these." He hesitated. "Carry on."

After Cain left, Nick pulled Felicia onto his lap to resume their interrupted make-out session. "You heard the man."

They faced each other and melted into a kiss. Nick tipped his head to one side and devoured Felicia's lips. They both savored the erotic smoothness as their tongues danced. Lips sealed together, they kissed pleasurably, fingers playing in the other's hair and holding each other close. There was no hurry to their kissing, no rush to their final destination.

They drew sexual energy from each other, kissing and letting their fingers brush lightly against personal hot zones. They had made this journey enough times to be familiar with the terrain, the kind of familiarity that brought a sense of comfort mixed with excitement. Each time, it added greater depth to their relationship and pulled them closer in spirit. They were now more able to read the other's emotions and sexual road signs.

Nick took in a quick breath when he felt Felicia's hand resting on his crotch, rubbing him through his pants while she kept her lips on his. Her caresses aroused him. He rested his hand on her braless breast, feeling her nipple harden through her shirt. Felicia broke their kiss and slid down to her knees. She unfastened his pants and reached in to fondle his hardness, increasing his desire.

Nick gasped when Felicia pulled his shorts down to let his cock spring free, then took him into her mouth. She hungrily sucked him while her hand slid slowly up and down his shaft, making him completely hard. He closed his eyes and enjoyed the feeling of Felicia's head bobbing up and down, working more of his length into her mouth.

Nick felt himself approaching the edge. He took Felicia's hands and pulled her to her feet. She quickly unfastened her slacks, pulled them down past her knees then bent over the nearby table. Nick took his place behind her and ran his fingers between her legs, noticing that she was already wet with desire. Felicia moaned softly as he slipped two fingers into her, gently manipulating her. She moved against his hand and loosened up the longer he played with her.

"Oh, hon," she softly said. "Take me now."

Nick easily slid into her from behind, pushing steadily until he was fully embedded in her wet sleeve. Felicia tossed her head back and moaned as she adjusted to his cock inside her. Nick jumped a bit when she clamped down on him with her inner muscles. He began thrusting slowly, relishing the feeling. Felicia rocked against him in the same rhythm, gyrating her hips with each backward push. Nick felt her hand slip between her legs when she reached down to rub her hard clit. The smell of her sex wafted to him, turning him on even more.

The closeness they had shared before their lovemaking combined with the sensual feel of Felicia's tight body to bring Nick to the brink. He felt his climax brewing and increased the speed and force of his hips. He gave a muffled groan when he swelled inside her. His climax triggered Felicia's own, her fingers rubbing her engorged clit as she came.

They stayed in position for a few moments, panting and catching their breath. Nick leaned over and wrapped his arms around Felicia's body. He planted light kisses on the back of her neck, and she giggled.

"That tickles," she whispered.

She placed her hand on Nick's sweaty cheek and exhaled a contented breath. "Damn, hon, you do that so good."

Nick moved a hand to her breast and gave a soft but firm squeeze. "So do you."

"Kind of a thrill, doin' it out here in the open."

Nick leaned in closer and kissed her cheek. "What was that you said about tough kick-ass women turning me on?"

She wiggled her butt against him. "Next time, I'll wear my black jumpsuit and you can wear your baggies."

Felicia fluffed her pillows for the third time that night then rolled onto her side. She closed her eyes and exhaled a deep breath, but sleep was beyond her grasp. Her mind was too active, replaying everything that had recently happened to disrupt the peaceful life she and Nick enjoyed.

A week ago, we were just livin' the dream, enjoyin' each other and havin' a good time. I keep thinkin' that if I hadn't insisted on goin' somewhere for a few days to do somethin' different, Nick wouldn't have run into his old girlfriend, or been accused of killin' her. I know he'll say it wasn't my fault, but I feel like I should've left well enough alone. If I had, he wouldn't have got beat up the other night, and we wouldn't be runnin' away from somethin' that was none of our doin'.

After another ten minutes of restlessness, she tossed back the covers and quietly slipped out of bed. Nick didn't share her insomnia and slept peacefully. She went downstairs to the kitchen, got a carton of orange juice from the fridge and took a few long swallows. She stood in the darkened room, absorbing the stillness, the only sound being the rhythmic ticking of the clock on the wall.

Felicia heard a noise coming from the sliding glass door that opened onto the deck. Her gaze quickly shifted in that direction and she heard what sounded like someone working on the lock. She set the carton on the counter then quietly crept into the dining room. She pulled back the floor-to-ceiling curtain a bit and peeked outside. She saw a man bent over, his hands using a lock pick on the door handle.

Felicia looked around for something to use as a weapon and settled on a foot-long heavy silver candlestick from the dining room table. She stood against the curtain near the door and waited, the candlestick poised over her head, ready to strike. The door slowly slid open and the intruder entered. When he was just inside, Felicia swung the candlestick forcefully, connecting with the man's right temple. He cried out in surprise and staggered a couple of steps.

She stepped forward to deliver another blow but the man regained his senses and raised his right arm to fend off the impact. He grabbed the candlestick with his other hand, wrestled it from Felicia's grip and tossed it aside. He charged at her but Felicia gave him a swift, hard kick in the stomach. He staggered backwards where he crashed into a sideboard, sending several pieces of glassware crashing onto the tile floor. Felicia pounced on him and delivered several hard blows to his abdomen before he pulled back his fist and connected with her jaw.

Felicia stumbled back, her head pounding and dizzy. The man poised his fist to deliver another blow but abruptly stopped. Felicia heard the sound of footsteps hurrying down the stairs, and the intruder ran through the open doorway into the night. Felicia leaned against the kitchen counter, rubbing her jaw and breathing deeply.

Nick ran into the room and turned on the light. "What the hell happened?"

"Break-in. Caught someone comin' in through the door from the deck."

Nick grabbed the phone and called 9-1-1. He surveyed the damage. "Did you get him?"

"Yeah. I clocked him upside the head with the candlestick and we roughhoused a little."

She looked at the broken items near the sideboard. "Dammit!"

"It's okay. We can replace that stuff."

Felicia pointed at one pile of broken glass. "That crystal dish belonged to my grandmother. That son of a bitch!"

Her gaze locked onto something shiny on the floor. She knelt down to examine it.

"Don't touch it," Nick said.

He went into the kitchen then returned with a pair of tongs. He picked up the item then held it out. It was a pendant with a large gold letter K spelled out in diamond chips, dangling from a broken heavy gold rope chain.

"Is that what I think it is?" Felicia asked.

"If you think it's Kristine Overman's necklace, then yes."

He put it back where it had been dropped and they both stood.

"Are you all right?" Nick asked.

Felicia flexed her shoulders and winced. "Yeah, I'm okay. Just shows I'm outta shape. Guess I should work out a little more."

"Right. You can moonlight as a bouncer at Alabama Jack's on country-western night. Should bring back fond memories."

She smacked his arm. "Hush."

Nick stepped over to the door and examined the lock. "Professional job. That guy didn't leave a mark. If you hadn't been down here, he could've gotten in and back out without leaving a trace."

"Except for plantin' evidence that makes you look guilty."

Nick looked at her. "I think someone just upped the ante." He stepped closer and examined her jaw where she had been punched. "Flex your jaw for me. Any pain?"

Felicia shook her head. "Just ringin' in my ears. I'll be all right."

Nick lightly ran his fingers over face. "Fascinating."

"You gettin' off on bruises now?"

"No, but he clocked you on the right side, which means he's left-handed." He hesitated. "Just like the killer. Before the cops get here, take some close-ups of that necklace, but don't touch it."

CHAPTER SIXTEEN

Daybreak had come early, on the tail end of a sleepless night. The heat and humidity were well on their way to living up to the Keys' reputation for late Spring — sultry with a chance of mugginess.

Nick and Felicia sat in a room at the police station, finalizing their reports on the midnight visitor to their home. They hadn't bothered trying to go back to sleep after the evidence techs left, and both were feeling a little testy from fatigue. Nick sipped coffee from a Styrofoam cup and made a face.

"Geez, no wonder the cops are so grumpy if this is what they have to drink."

"Maybe you could open a gourmet coffee stand in the lobby," Felicia drily suggested. "Might be a big hit with the prisoners, too."

"Ha ha."

They took their reports to Cain's office. He stood as they entered then addressed Felicia.

"How are you feeling, slugger?"

"I'll live," she said.

They took seats and Cain scanned their statements. "I sent that necklace to the lab for a fingerprint check, along with the candlestick the guy grabbed during the struggle. Anything you'd care to tell me before they send me the report?"

"They won't find my prints on that necklace," Nick said. "Felicia's, either."

"I'm sure they won't. Anything else you can tell me about it?"

Nick looked at him. "It belonged to Kristine Overman. She was wearing it the night she confronted me in the casino, but it wasn't on that inventory your friend provided."

"Yeah, I checked that, too. I did find out that the medical examiner noted an abrasion on the back of her neck, consistent with a chain being torn off during a struggle."

"You think Overman paid someone to leave it in our place to make you look guilty?" Felicia asked.

"No doubts in my mind," Nick said.

Cain slowly shook his head. "Planting evidence. Haven't seen that trick in about a month. Someone's desperate."

"That backs up our working theory," Nick said. "He knows who did it and he's covering for them. When Overman called Bianco and offered him money to drop the hammer on me, he said he'd provide the proof. Do you suppose that necklace is what he had in mind?"

"It fits with everything else he's pulled on you," Cain replied.

"There's something else," Nick said. "Whoever broke in and punched Felicia last night was apparently left-handed. I suspect that Kristine's killer was, too."

"I'll add that to my notes."

"Are you still bringing in DeGarmo for questioning in Raul's drug arrest?"

Cain looked at the clock on the wall. "Should be here within the hour. Want to watch?"

Nick stood. "No, I'll wait for the special on *Dateline*."

He and Felicia drove back to Key Largo with the top down on the Mustang. The breeze felt good as it blew over them. Felicia looked at the oceanside scenery through a pair of large sunglasses and Nick drummed his fingers on the steering wheel in time with the jazz playing on the car stereo. Neither of them said much during the ride.

When they reached town, Nick pulled into the lot at Doc's

Diner, a local hangout that was only open for breakfast and lunch. While not in the tour guides as a must-do dining experience, the cuisine was hearty homemade fare, definitely not for the calorie- or cholesterol-conscious. They placed their orders then sipped coffee.

"You been awful quiet since we left Ted's office," Felicia noted.

"You weren't exactly a Chatty Cathy on the ride back, either."

"Just thinkin'." She rubbed her jaw. "Damn, that guy had a hard left. Ain't taken a hit like that in a long time."

"Don't worry, you're still the toughest broad this side of the West Indies."

Felicia laughed and lightly smacked his arm. "You haven't called me that lately." She paused. "I've kinda missed it."

Nick gazed adoringly at her, then took her hand. "I haven't had to call you that in a long time, angel."

She gave a shy smile and cast her gaze downward while brushing back a lock of hair from her face. "That's okay. I like angel better, tough guy."

"Do you remember when you started calling me that?"

She looked into his eyes. "When we worked together in England." She hesitated. "When I called you that the first time, though, it wasn't a compliment."

Nick's eyebrows arched. "It wasn't?"

Felicia shook her head. "Our team finished an op and things didn't go like they were supposed to. When we were debriefing, you got your ass up in the air and chewed everyone out for bein' careless. I think I said *tough guy* just to be a smartass."

Nick laughed. "When did the meaning change?"

Felicia gave him a dreamy-eyed gaze. "When I started fallin' for you. I figured out that tough exterior you like to show off masked somethin' else."

"What was I hiding with it?"

She squeezed his hand. "A little boy who had to take on the bullies on the playground and give back as good as he got."

Nick grinned. "I never could hide things from you."

Their orders arrived and they ate. Felicia picked at the fresh fruit plate she had ordered while Nick dived into a platter of scrambled eggs, sausage links, and hash browns.

Felicia looked at him in awe. "I never seen you eat that much for breakfast."

Nick chased his food with coffee. "Fatigue. When I'm tired, I get hungry."

Felicia speared a strawberry and munched it while her eyes wandered to the TV mounted above the cash register. She gasped, reached over and clutched Nick's hand.

"Hon, check out the TV."

Nick turned around and looked at the screen. J.P. Overman was holding a press conference. They walked to the counter to hear what was being said. Overman was dressed in one of his expensive suits and looked as grandiose as he could, matching his pompous delivery.

"As many of you know, my youngest daughter, Kristine, was the victim of a brutal murder over a week ago," he said. "It occurred on a popular tourist destination called the Gold Flamingo, a gambling establishment operated by a man of less than reputable pedigree named Rock Bianco, a man with known criminal ties. To date, her murder remains unsolved. The investigation was entrusted to the Fort Lauderdale police, who have not been diligent in their sworn duties to apprehend the man responsible for this tragedy."

He stopped to gesture at a monitor that showed a glamour shot of Kristine Overman.

"This is my daughter, Kristine. God knows I love all of my children equally, but she was the special light in my life. The police had a very likely suspect in custody, a man who had every reason to snuff out this precious life at far too young an age, the man you now see before you."

Nick's eyes widened when he saw his face on the screen.

"They chose to let him go," Overman continued, his voice escalating. "He apparently fabricated evidence that the authorities, the people we entrust with our safety, chose to believe over actual facts. This man, Nick Seven of Key Largo, has a well-documented history of violence. He is a former CIA operative and has killed before, supposedly with the blessing of the United States government. My own investigation has uncovered facts that undercut that defense. To allow this man to remain free is an insult to the decent God-fearing Americans that have made this country great. You may blame Broward County prosecutor Frank McCorkle for that. It was his decision not to pursue charges in spite of overwhelming evidence."

He paused to take a sip of water from the glass on the lectern. "Today, I am making a personal appeal, in front of you good citizens, to the Florida State Attorney General to take over the investigation, and to appoint a Special Prosecutor to bring my daughter's killer to justice. I will now take your questions."

Felicia firmly gripped Nick's arm and spoke in a low panicked voice. "Hon, what the hell do we do about this?"

Nick stared at the screen, recalling what he had heard about Overman's on-camera meltdowns. "Wait for the other shoe to drop."

"Mr. Overman," one of the reporters began, "is it true that the SEC has begun an investigation into your business dealings with the Turkish government?"

Overman's gaze narrowed and his face tightened noticeably as the camera zoomed in for a close-up. His left eye twitched and he stared at the man.

"Are you really a reporter?" he angrily demanded in a loud voice. "Did you not understand the purpose of this press briefing when you were invited here today? Are you that stupid?" He smirked. "You phony media types make me ill, always looking for opportunities to humiliate and embarrass me so you can sell more copies of your worthless writing."

"But is it true . . ." the reporter continued.

"Enough!" Overman snapped. "I will not stand here and allow you to bother me with these nuisance questions that are totally inappropriate. We're here to discuss the steps I'm taking to bring my daughter's killer to justice, not some government witch hunt into my private business affairs."

Other reporters shouted out questions but Overman abruptly walked out of the room. The on-air commentator appeared on the screen to recap what had just happened.

"Meltdown," Nick said.

CHAPTER SEVENTEEN

Ted Cain leaned against the wall of the interrogation room, his arms folded over his chest and his steely eyes taking in the man sitting at the table. Willie DeGarmo was just over six feet tall, husky, with thinning brown-and-gray hair. His jowly face and baggy eyes bore the evidence of his more than passing acquaintance with the bottle. One of Cain's senior deputies, a no-nonsense former Miami cop named Ferguson, sat nearby with his notepad and pen at the ready.

"Let's try this again," Cain said. "We have you on a security camera planting marijuana in a car yesterday morning at a convenience store in north Key Largo. Who put you up to it?"

"Wasn't me," DeGarmo said. "You got the wrong guy."

"No, it was you, all right," Ferguson said. "We got a nice clear picture, along with the license plate on your car."

DeGarmo shook his head. "Typical hick cops. You got some José-come-lately running drugs and you try to pin it on a fellow police officer. You'd do better chasing down expired fishing licenses."

Cain and Ferguson exchanged glances.

"How did you know the owner of the car is a Latino?" Cain asked.

DeGarmo cast his gaze down.

"We've got more than just your plate number," Cain continued. "You weren't very careful when you handled the package. You left your fingerprints all over it. That's pretty sloppy for an experienced cop from the big bad city."

"There's also an ID from a witness," Ferguson added. "But she's Cuban, so you probably think she's lying."

DeGarmo was silent. Cain opened a file folder and flipped through a few pages.

"I spoke with your former squad commander, and he sent me your file," he said while referencing a page. "Looks like internal affairs had you on speed dial. Fifteen complaints, mostly for excessive force and harassment."

"Nuisance complaints from people I collared," DeGarmo said, looking at Ferguson. "You used to work the Miami beat. You know how those people are when they get arrested. Everybody wants to holler *police brutality*. First English words they teach 'em after they sneak across the border."

"I noticed that gash and bruise on the side of your head," Cain said. "How did you get that?"

"Came home drunk and walked into a door," DeGarmo said.

"Are you sure you didn't get it during a home invasion last night, when you were caught by a woman who beaned you with a silver candlestick?"

DeGarmo exhaled a slow breath. "Never happened. I was home last night."

"Then how did your fingerprints end up on that same candlestick, the one you wrestled away from her?"

DeGarmo remained silent and examined the wood grain on the table.

"You also left a nice set of prints on the lock you picked to get into that home," Ferguson said, "along with a clear thumbprint on the jewelry you dropped inside. No offense, but for a former Miami cop, you don't seem to be too bright."

DeGarmo raised his gaze to look at Cain. "I'm assuming there's some form of *quid pro quo* in this."

"What could a washed-up cop with a record like yours have to offer?" Cain asked.

DeGarmo shrugged. "The name of the person who sent me down here."

"We're listening."

DeGarmo laughed softly. "You get your prosecutor over here, then maybe. Until then, I'm deaf and dumb."

"Interesting choice of words," Cain said then addressed Ferguson. "Get him out of here, then have this room fumigated."

Ferguson led DeGarmo into the hallway and instructed a deputy to take him to a holding cell. Cain stopped Ferguson, speaking in a low voice. "You told me you couldn't find a witness at that mini-mart."

Ferguson shrugged. "DeGarmo doesn't know that. You gonna get Garcia over here to talk deal with him?"

Cain looked at his watch. "Ya know, my schedule's pretty tight this afternoon. I may find time to call him tomorrow, the day after. We can hold DeGarmo for seventy-two hours before we have to arraign him. Make sure he's comfortable."

Ferguson chuckled. "That's not bad for a couple of hick cops."

Nick sat at his desk, his gaze fixed on the computer screen while he used the mouse to fast-forward and replay the video action. He had accessed the archives from the local TV stations of J.P. Overman's previous public dealings with the media, and absorbed his responses to certain questions, along with his involuntary reactions.

When one of them asks him a question he doesn't want to answer, his left eye begins to twitch, then he stares at the person before responding, like he did this morning. Reminds me of the sleepy-eyed look a croc gives its prey before it moves in for the kill. His voice gets louder, and he repeats certain words, like phony media, parasites, liars, and harassment. The man's a Freudian delight.

Felicia entered the room and looked over his shoulder.

"You've been watchin' that trash talk for over an hour. You'll rot your brain. What're you hopin' to find?"

"I think I found it. Whenever Overman gets a question that wanders from his agenda, he goes into these long rants about how everyone's out to get him. Then he brags about his accomplishments to take the focus off of the question."

"Sounds like a sociopath to me."

"At least. I always suspected there was something not quite right about him."

She perched on the edge of the desk and let her leg swing freely. "I thought you wrote him off as a rich snob."

"I never saw him go into rambling diatribes like he does in these press briefings, but he made more than a few inappropriate remarks."

"About what?"

Nick rocked his chair. "About anyone who didn't agree with him, and he was especially unkind toward immigrants." He hesitated. "Always made me cringe."

"You said he does a lot of business with foreign countries. If he's so pro-America, why deal with them?"

Nick looked at her. "It's where the real money is."

He answered his ringing cell phone. "Seven."

"This is Bill Ceretta. I got that information we talked about. You gonna be around tonight?"

"I'll be at Cricket's all evening. What time?"

"Eight, eight-thirty. You can pick up the first round."

"Is this worthwhile stuff?"

Ceretta chuckled. "You won't be disappointed."

Nick disconnected then set the phone on the desk. "Ceretta came through with the goods. He's coming to the club tonight."

"What're you gonna do with whatever he found out?"

Nick stared at the image on the screen. "As much damage as I can."

CHAPTER EIGHTEEN

Darkness stretched from the Gulf shoreline to eternity, obscuring the distant fingers of the Everglades with a blanket of black. The cresting full moon played hide-and-seek with grayish wisps of clouds forecasting an overnight storm. The darkness was interrupted by a handful of flashing blue and green lights emanating from the boats of a few brave souls tempting the storm gods on the horizon. The breeze picked up as it blew through the outdoor deck at Cricket's, causing the patrons to clutch their plastic cups and paper napkins lest they become gone with the wind.

Nick and Felicia stared into the nighttime view while sipping their drinks. Nick had been unusually subdued after witnessing Overman's on-air throwing down of the gauntlet. His mind had been far from inactive, in spite of the fatigue he still felt from the night before. He had tried to put on a positive front for Felicia, but knew deep down that she wasn't buying any of it.

He glanced at her across the table. *I know she's taking this whole thing pretty hard, and I have no right to impose my problems on her. Felicia keeps dropping little hints and questions about my relationship with Kristine Overman, but I've told her everything. I learned a long time ago that she could see through any barrier I put up to mask what's really going on in my mind.*

Nick reached over to squeeze Felicia's hand and get her attention. She faced him and offered a shy smile.

"What?" she asked.

"Nothing special. Just wanted to tell you how much I

appreciate you."

"What brought that on?"

"Do I need a reason to tell you that?"

"No, I guess not. I appreciate you, too." She hesitated. "Hon, I'm sorry if I've been snippy lately. Guess all this stuff is botherin' me more than I should let it."

"I'm the one who should apologize for dragging you into my problem."

She gave him a curious look. "It isn't just your problem. It's our problem, because we're a team. Did you forget that?"

"No, I didn't forget, but thank you for reminding me."

They were interrupted by Bill Ceretta approaching the table. He pointed at an empty chair.

"Got room for a thirsty party crasher?"

"What kept you?"

Ceretta took a seat and Nick signaled to a passing server to take his drink order. She returned a few minutes later with a Sour Apple Martini. Ceretta took a sip then opened a manila envelope he'd brought with him.

"As promised," he said while removing a thick sheaf of papers which he set on the table. "J.P. Overman, the hidden years."

Nick eagerly grabbed the pages and skimmed through them, looking at the highlights. *Wow.* "Is this stuff reliable?"

"Horse's mouth. Pretty wild, huh?"

"I'll say. Considering the grudge you have against Overman because of what he did to your family, why aren't you using this yourself?"

Ceretta looked into his glass. "You read the papers down here. Strictly non-partisan and a-political. They don't print anything that would piss off the tourists and advertisers. I asked my editor for a pass so I could write a series on this, and he said no way. I can't use it, so I'm giving it to you."

"You write a daily blog in addition to your weekly column.

144

Why don't you post it there?"

"That blog is owned by the newspaper. If I posted this, it would go under my byline, and is therefore considered news. If someone questioned me, I'd have to verify my sources."

"What am I supposed to do with it? I'm not a member of the press."

Ceretta shook his head, sighed and retrieved one of the pages. He took a pen from his pocket, scrawled on the page then slid it back.

"If it kills me, I'm gonna get you into the twenty-first century before the next millennium," he said. "Here's the online address for a chat board made up of people Overman screwed over for fun and profit. That's a dummy account I set up, along with my password. Use it."

"Do you think that'll get the word out to enough people?"

"When anything juicy is posted on there, it gets recycled on other forums. Figure it out."

Nick sat back and sipped his scotch. *It could work.* "Felicia, what do you think about this craziness?"

"I think it's worth a shot," she said. "Just because you don't spend your days surfin' the 'net doesn't mean no one else does. Use whatever you can to bury that asshole."

"It appears I'm not the only one holding a grudge," Ceretta commented. "After what I've read lately, I'd think you'd jump at the chance to stick it to that prick."

Nick smirked. "I want to stick it to him, but until he started this latest barrage, I didn't want to sink to his level."

"But now?"

Nick looked at him. "The gloves are off."

Ceretta grinned. "Welcome to the good fight." He took a sip. "Not to pry, but I saw his latest episode of *Screw the Press* this morning. Are you worried about him calling on the AG to appoint a hired gun to come after you?"

Nick thought for a moment. "A little, but I've already had

a talk with my attorney. He thinks it's all smoke and mirrors, just another tactic to draw attention from the real issue."

"Which is?"

"Overman knows who killed his daughter but he wants to hang me for it."

Ceretta downed his drink then stood up. "I hope you nail his ass to the wall with a solid gold spike. If you need anything else, call me."

Nick went back to reading the papers, absorbing more details this time.

"Well?" Felicia asked at length. "You gonna share, or is it classified?"

"Maybe it should be. I can see why Overman kept this hidden. He attended a boarding school in Boston for the rich and pampered after he was booted out of a private school in Palm Beach."

"Who gets kicked out of a pay-for-play school? Was he a disciplinary problem?"

"In a way. The official reason cited below-average grades, emotional instability and continuous fights with his classmates."

"How old was he?"

"Fifteen." Nick flipped to the next page. "He only lasted one semester in Boston before they expelled him for the same reasons. His old man sent him to a military school in Pensacola to straighten him out, but he washed out of there, too. He spent the next two years at home with private tutors until he earned a GED."

"What about college?"

Nick scanned the page. "According to this, J.P. attended Florida State, majoring in business, but there's no record of him graduating." He looked at another page. "But his press page states that he graduated *cum laude* from their school of business."

"What kind of grade point average?"

Nick looked at her. "It doesn't say." He read a notation scrawled next to it. "Ceretta put a note in here. He made an inquiry but the university said they weren't legally permitted to comment."

"Not legally permitted?"

"Translation—Overman's attorney filed a restraining order." He continued reading. "Here's something interesting. Five years ago, he took leave from his company and checked into a private hospital in Tampa for a month. His press corps said it was for exhaustion, but insiders at the hospital claim he was a guest in the psych ward. If he spent time in a mental health facility, that's something he'd have to keep hidden."

"Because he was stressed out?"

Nick shook his head. "Because people might think he's mentally incompetent. You know the kind of damage a thing like that can do to a high-profile public figure. His decisions would come under scrutiny and his big money clients might bail."

"Let me see if I get this so far," Felicia said. "His people put together a fake life, complete with a phony school record, but no mention of his alleged mental health issues."

"You're following along beautifully."

She tucked one leg under her then cradled her glass, settling in for the long haul. "You've got me hooked. What's the rest of the story?"

Nick flipped to another page. "This one's about his family. J.P. Junior tried to enlist in the Navy after high school but he didn't pass the psych eval. They said he was emotionally unstable and exhibited tendencies toward explosive anger outbursts. In other words, a grenade with the pin pulled. He's been arrested twice for domestic violence but the victims declined to press charges each time. He was also hit with a paternity suit, but it was withdrawn."

"Think those women were bought off?"

"I can guarantee it." He read further down the page. "Mental instability isn't the only thing that runs in the family. When the old man's first wife filed for divorce, there were hints that he was physically abusive, but she never pressed charges, either."

"Didn't want to tarnish the family's good name?"

"That isn't something one talks about in country club society, and it probably would've cut into her alimony."

"You said that was what he did to his first wife. What about his current spouse?"

"Apparently, the only time she's seen in public is on his arm at some black-tie function. According to the newspaper and magazine spreads, they're all one big happy family."

Felicia laughed. "A happy family of psychos livin' behind a curtain made of money."

"Hey, if you've got it, might as well do yourself some good with it."

"Didn't you say he had a daughter who OD'ed a few years ago?"

Nick flipped through the pages. "Yeah, Brittany Overman. There isn't much about her in here, but I remember when it happened. That was front page stuff for a while."

Felicia paused for a few moments. "What did you find in there about Kristine?"

Nick looked at her over the papers. "You really want to hear it?"

"Hon, I'm not bothered that you two had a fling, because it was over before I got here. It isn't a touchy subject for me. Whatever you find in that file might put a stop to this foolishness and let us get on with our lives."

Nick grinned and felt like another brick had fallen from the wall he had built around his heart. "Okay. According to this, Kristine made a stab at being a co-ed at Vanderbilt, up in

Nashville. She dropped out before the end of her freshman year."

"Homesick?"

Nick shook his head. "An allegation involving sexually inappropriate behavior."

"Someone harassed her?"

"Nope. She set her sights on her English lit professor and wouldn't let up. She apparently hounded the poor bastard until he had to file a restraining order against her. Almost cost him his tenure and his marriage."

"You thinkin' love affair gone bad?"

"They probably had a fling and when the guy decided to end it, that wasn't what she wanted to hear." He paused. "Just like her old man after I proved my innocence."

"Along with everything else. From what I've read, anytime the press questions him about somethin' that doesn't look right, he claims it isn't his fault."

"That's one thing about that clan—they're never to blame, for anything."

He dropped the pages on the table then took a drink.

"What're you gonna do with that?" Felicia asked.

"Starting tomorrow, we become a couple of social media stalkers."

Felicia chuckled. "Can't wait."

Nick stretched and yawned. "Man, after today, I'm ready to crash hard."

"Me, too. I wonder what Ted found out about Raul's problem when he questioned that guy today?"

Nick's attention was caught by Ted Cain approaching the table with his wife, an attractive middle-aged blonde with a trim figure and natural tan, wearing a tropical print sarong. "Speak of the devil."

He stood when they approached and offered a smile. "Hello, Peg. Haven't seen you in a while."

They took seats. "Afraid I don't get out much lately." She turned to Felicia and smiled. "How have you been, Felicia?"

"I'm doing okay, thank you. Are you still working at Founder's Hospital?"

Peg groaned. "More than I'd like to sometimes. When they say there's a nursing shortage down here, they aren't kidding."

Nick signaled for a server to take care of his guests. After their drinks arrived, Cain began the conversation.

"If you don't mind discussing a little business after hours, I wanted to give you an update."

Nick sipped his scotch. "I'm curious about what you found out."

"At first, DeGarmo denied everything, claimed we had the wrong guy, you know, the usual bullshit. When we told him our evidence placed him at both scenes, he caved. He said if Garcia offered him a good deal, he'd be willing to snitch on who gave the orders."

"Do you think he'll deliver the goods?"

"This guy knows how to work the system. When he figured out we weren't playing around, he decided to save his sorry ass."

"What else did you get from him?"

"A definite distaste for Latino immigrants."

"I guess I'm not surprised. Is Garcia going for a deal?"

Ted took a sip. "I haven't sprung it on him yet. I'm letting DeGarmo chill in lock-up for a day or two."

"If he's willing to implicate Overman as the brains, why not move on it?"

"I want to dig deeper and make a stronger case before we go forward. Overman has a billion-dollar war chest and lawyers racking up billable hours in two time zones. You know he could tie us up for years with motions and appeals."

"I hear that, but why do you want to take him on? His

problem is with me, not you. You might be setting yourself up for the big fall."

"If he told DeGarmo to come into my jurisdiction and commit a handful of felonies, he crossed a line." He paused. "I also figured you're up to something, and wanted to give you time to work on it."

Nick grinned. "Thanks."

"What are you planning?"

"A counterstrike. I got some juicy info on my nemesis courtesy of Bill Ceretta, the reporter. You know him?"

Cain got a sour look on his face. "We're acquainted. During my last election, he thought he was being funny with a piece he wrote about how I handled some squatters down on Little Torch Key."

"I don't recall that. What happened?"

Cain took a drink. "The county commissioners had a complaint from a guy who owned an abandoned mobile home park, one that was wiped out by a hurricane. Some refugees set up camp there, and he wanted them gone so he could sell the property. I was doing my job, but Ceretta wrote a sarcastic column about it."

Peg giggled. "Didn't he give you the cutest nickname, dear?"

Ted stared at her. "Hard-hearted Ted, the beast of the Keys. Thanks for reminding me."

Nick and Felicia laughed along with Ted's wife.

"Don't take it personally," Nick said. "Can't be the first time a reporter used you like a dartboard."

"No, but it doesn't mean I liked it."

Nick looked into his glass. "After what's been happening to me lately, I know just how you feel."

CHAPTER NINETEEN

Cain was at his desk the following morning, sipping coffee while reviewing reports of the previous night's activities. There was a knock on his open door and he looked up to see Manuel Garcia, the Monroe County Prosecutor walking in. Despite the nearly constant humidity of the Keys, Garcia always chose to wear a suit and tie. He eased his thin frame into a chair across from Cain's desk and didn't waste time on *how-about-this-weather*.

"Are you holding a man named DeGarmo on charges of drug possession and breaking and entering?"

Ted eyed him warily for a moment. "So happens we are. How did you know?"

"I had a call from one of J.P. Overman's attorneys. He heard DeGarmo was brought here for questioning and no one's seen him since. When were you going to tell me about his arrest?"

Ted glanced down for a few moments. "We're still gathering evidence, and I have three days to make a formal charge."

"I'm aware of that, but I don't like being blindsided by an attorney who makes more on retainer than I do in a year. You should've told me, Ted."

"Because he's connected to Overman?"

Garcia's gaze narrowed. "What's that supposed to mean?"

"If DeGarmo was some punk we picked up for burglary and drug possession, you would've sent one of your assistants over here. When you heard the name J.P. Overman, you became interested. What's going on, Manny?"

Garcia paused. "Okay, I'll admit it caught my attention. He's a powerful man and well-connected within the state judicial system. What kind of evidence do you have?"

"We can place him at the scene of the break-in at Nick Seven's home, and we have a video of him planting drugs in Raul Barba's car just before the anonymous call came in. His fingerprints were found on the drugs he planted, and also on some items at Seven's place. When we pressed him about it, DeGarmo copped to everything. He also said if you gave him a sweetheart deal, he'd implicate Overman for setting up both crimes."

"Did he specifically say it was on Overman's orders?"

Ted hesitated. "Not specifically, but he's part of his private security team. We made the connection."

Garcia let out a slow deep breath. "Not a very strong one." He tapped his fingers on the arm of the chair. "Do you really think he's telling the truth?"

"I think he won't provide names until he gets what he wants. This guy is the textbook definition of a dirty cop and he knows which buttons to push."

"I noticed that Nick Seven seems to be the common thread."

"And I know your personal feelings about him," Ted interrupted. "Whenever he gets jammed up in a real problem, you're quick to point out that he probably brought it on himself."

Garcia's face tensed up a bit. "I'll admit that in the past I thought any bad luck that came his way was his own doing."

"In fact, I recall a quote you used once upon a time. Something about *That guy's like a lightning rod in a hurricane when it comes to attracting trouble.* Coming back to you?"

Garcia cast his gaze down. "Possibly a poor choice of words in the heat of the moment. What I'm trying to ascertain from you is his involvement in this. I've been following

Overman's accusations about his daughter's murder, and his request for an independent investigation."

"Is there a question in there, or are you fishing?"

Garcia gave him a hard, penetrating look. "I just want to know if we're harboring a killer."

Ted returned his steely gaze. "No, we are not. Nick proved his innocence to the Broward County prosecutor, but Overman isn't letting it go. I think this recent series of events might uncover something bigger."

Garcia sat quietly for a few moments. "Has DeGarmo been given his Miranda rights, including his right to have an attorney present?"

"Yes, and he waived them, in writing."

"Why would he do that if he's on Overman's payroll?"

"My guess? DeGarmo doesn't think they'll bail him out and he wants to make the best deal he can for himself."

"Overman's attorney said he's coming down here this afternoon, and he'll expect a sit-down with his supposed client. That means I need to make a deal with DeGarmo before they make him a better offer to remain silent." He slowly shook his head. "If there was only some way to make him unavailable until after his attorney leaves . . ."

Ted tried to hide a smile. He picked up the phone and punched in a number. "Fergie, come in here."

A few minutes later, Lieutenant Ferguson came in. Ted grabbed a pad from his desk, wrote on it, then tore off the top sheet and handed it to him.

Ferguson looked at it. "What's this?"

"The transfer request you asked for this morning, to move DeGarmo to the prisoner's ward at Founder's Hospital."

"Why are we moving him to the hospital?"

Cain looked at him. "You told me that after breakfast, DeGarmo complained of stomach and chest pains. I can't have an ill prisoner in the general population. Don't you remember?"

Ferguson nodded. "Yeah, that's what I said. He told us he wasn't feeling too good after chow. I'll get right on this."

"Be sure to tell the Doc to do a thorough work-up, you know, lab tests, CT scan, the whole ticket. Make sure he gets a private room, with a deputy on duty."

Ferguson left and Garcia let out a deep sigh. "What do I tell his attorney when he gets here?"

Ted looked at him. "Tell him there was a clerical error and your county sheriff is looking into it. Tell him it happens all the time with hick cops who still do things the old school way."

Nick stood on the deck under the mid-day sun while Felicia worked inside on the computer. They had gotten an early start on their smear campaign by taking the information Ceretta had provided and working it into smaller posts that hinted at something larger to come.

Nick had decided to use the teaser approach—drop embarrassing bits of innuendo a few morsels at a time, see if it found its way to a larger market, then fire the big missile when the time was right. While reviewing the info they were posting, Nick ran across something that intrigued him, one that required clarification. He called Bill Ceretta.

"It's Seven," he said when Ceretta answered. "I wanted to thank you for what you dropped off last night. It's great stuff."

"I have no idea what you're talking about."

Nick laughed. "Oh, yeah, I forgot. Should I nickname you Deep Throat?"

"Ya know, I always admired that guy for coming forward and blowing the whistle on Nixon. What do you need?"

"What else can you tell me about Overman's son?"

Ceretta chuckled. "You mean Junior? He's a total waste of space. Never worked a day in his life. He spends all his time partying and figuring out new ways to spend daddy's money."

"I hear he likes to smack his women around and he's been arrested a couple of times, but none of his victims pressed charges. You know anything about that?"

"One of Big Daddy's lawyers always showed up with a fat check and a non-disclosure agreement. Rumor has it that there was also an unplanned pregnancy once upon a time."

"Anything come of it?"

Ceretta paused. "There aren't any little Overman's running around, if that's what you mean. It'd be a safe bet the old man's money was at work again."

Damn! "Thanks. I'll be in touch."

Nick disconnected then went inside, stopping in the kitchen to refill his iced tea. He looked at the area where the fight had taken place a couple of nights earlier. The sideboard was missing a few pieces of china and glassware.

Felicia was really upset about that heirloom from her grand-mother getting destroyed. She has so little from home. I don't have too many things from my own family, either, only my dad's watch and my mom's engagement ring. That's about all, aside from a few family photos that I don't look at very often. I travel light. I guess that came in handy in the CIA, since I was seldom in the same place for very long.

He went to the den, where Felicia was busy at the computer. "How goes it?"

"Pretty good, considerin' we only started postin' things a few hours ago. It's already had more than a thousand hits."

Nick sipped his tea. "Is that a good thing?"

Felicia looked up at him. "You really should get into this tech stuff. It would open up a whole new world for you."

"You sound like a commercial. Next you'll tell me I can't live without that newfangled invention called color TV."

"Don't be such a smart-ass." She pulled up a screen she had been working on. "Here's a breakdown of what I've posted so far. I covered his school record and his apparent lack of a college degree. Where do you want to go next?"

Nick looked over her shoulder. "That stuff about his first marriage, his son's attempt at joining the Navy, and Junior's domestic violence complaints." He hesitated. "There's something we can add to that last item."

"Like what?"

"Payoffs to not press charges, and Overman paying for an abortion."

Felicia let out a low whistle. "That's heavy stuff. What's the big bombshell you're savin'?"

"His time in that mental health facility in Tampa."

Felicia paused for a moment. "What about that thing with Kristine in college?"

Nick sat in a wicker armchair and thought for a few moments. He tried to focus on the real target, the guy who was personally attacking him. While his family's adventures could be considered fair game, as they were in the mainstream media, Nick was hesitant to besmirch the reputation of someone he was accused of killing.

"Let's hold off on using that for now."

Felicia turned in her seat to look at him. "Havin' second thoughts?"

"Not really. Overman has used my late wife's murder to make me look bad, but I'm not certain I want to use his daughter's death for the same purpose. He's also suing me and it's still an open police investigation. If, by some miracle, the cops are actually closing in on a suspect, I don't want to muddy the waters. Does that make sense?"

"Hon, Overman's makin' damn sure they aren't lookin' at anyone else. You sure there isn't another reason?"

"Like what?"

She paused. "Sentimental reasons?"

Nick looked at her for a few moments. "No sentiment, angel. She isn't the one causing us all this trouble. He is."

Felicia cast her gaze down and smiled shyly. "I'm glad to hear you say *us*. I expected you to say *me*."

Nick walked over to her and placed his fingertips under her chin, raising her gaze to meet his. "It's the same thing." He paused for a moment. "I just realized something. In all of the press coverage of the murder, there's been no mention of the drugs the cops found. Why do you suppose that is?"

Felicia shrugged. "Overman got to the cops and made sure they didn't release that detail?"

"Damn likely. Save that for future use."

He recalled what he had been thinking about before he came into the room. He took Felicia's hands and prompted her to stand. He pulled her in for a tight hug.

"I think you've been working too hard on this and you're due for a break."

"I won't argue with you."

They went to the deck after getting fresh drinks. Nick adjusted the umbrella over the table to deflect the sun.

Felicia scanned the surrounding area through dark glasses. "Pretty day. They said it was gonna rain."

Nick looked skyward. "Just a few clouds up there. We'll probably get our daily sprinkle then it'll move on." He sipped his tea. "Felicia, I feel bad about that piece of glassware that got broken the other night when you tangled ass with DeGarmo."

She looked down. "Hey, no big deal. It's just a dish, right?" She hesitated. "But it did belong to my grandmama. She kept it on a table, filled with candy. Whenever us kids came over, she let us sneak some and pretended like she didn't see it. I really miss her."

"I can see why it has sentimental value."

"When I left home and wanted to take it with me, my mom didn't want me to."

"Why?"

Felicia shrugged. "Guess she thought since I was movin' all over the world, I couldn't be trusted with it." She looked at Nick. "I was close to Grammy Eloise since I was the oldest, and I got pissed at my mom for sayin' what she did."

"She must've listened, since you had it."

Felicia shook her head. "Not without a fight. If I tell her it got destroyed in my custody, she'll never let me hear the end of it."

He sat back and viewed the scenery. *Maybe I can make up for her loss.*

Brannigan and Cortez entered Kruger's office, braced for their daily spanking. Kruger made no effort to conceal his irritation and impatience.

"What progress have you two made on the Overman killing?" he demanded.

"We talked to the guy who followed her from the casino the night she was killed," Cortez replied. "All he'd say was he was there to meet Kristine Overman because she was a customer."

"Sounds promising. Did he say who beat the daylights out of him?"

Cortez shook his head. "He's sticking with his *I-slipped-and-fell* story. With the amount of drugs in his possession, he knows he's looking at hard time. After he regains his senses, he might name names to get a better deal."

Kruger focused his attention on Brannigan. "I heard you two paid a call on Rock Bianco. What did he have to say?"

"How did you know we went out there?" Brannigan asked.

"The legal system is an amazing thing, Phil. When attorneys feel that their clients are being threatened by the police, they're allowed to call people like me to bitch about it."

Brannigan hesitated. "Yeah, we spoke with Bianco, but we didn't threaten him."

"Really? What would you call implying that he could be charged with assault on that Parks guy if he didn't cooperate with your homicide investigation?"

Brannigan and Cortez exchanged uneasy glances.

"Okay, maybe we hinted that Parks was pressing charges," Cortez said. "Last I checked, we were allowed to use subterfuge on a suspect."

"Is Bianco a suspect, Ray? It isn't a trick question."

"No, he isn't. We were just trying to catch a break, since no one else is talking."

Kruger dropped a folded newspaper on the desk in front of them. "No one except J.P. Overman. He's still calling for a special prosecutor to take over the investigation."

"All things considered," Brannigan said, "that might not be the worst that could happen."

Kruger gave him an icy stare. "I'm not going down like the Titanic. This is our case, and we'll solve it without some political hack from the AG's office riding shotgun. Am I making myself clear?"

They both nodded then left. When they were in the squad room, Cortez took his jacket from the back of his chair and slipped into it.

"You up for a road trip?" he asked.

"To where?" Brannigan replied.

"Key Largo. Seven is in this up to his eyeballs. It's time to find out what he's hiding."

Brannigan held up his hands. "Whoa. Bad move, partner. We were ordered to stay away from him."

Cortez looked at him. "You know what? I don't really care. If you don't want to come along, fine."

Brannigan exhaled a long breath. "I'll drive."

CHAPTER TWENTY

Nick paced in the living room with the phone at his ear, listening to his attorney update him on his case. Grand told him that the civil suit for wrongful death was still in limbo, and he had been researching laws regarding defamation and slander.

"What about that special prosecutor Overman requested? Is the AG going to give it to him?"

"I reached out to one of my former junior partners who now works in their office," Grand said. "Off the record, he said it doesn't appear likely."

"Doesn't appear likely? I don't take much comfort in that."

"Until we hear something more definitive, it's the best we have."

"Why isn't he going for it, considering how much trouble Overman could cause for him?"

Grand laughed softly. "The AG isn't a big fan. Apparently, Overman offered to finance his last campaign but he didn't want to be indebted to him."

"Wow, a politician with a backbone," Nick said. "I'm glad I lived to see this day. What about this online harassment he's engaging in? Can't we do something about that?"

"My sources tell me someone's already doing something about it. You wouldn't know anything about that, would you, Nicholas?"

Nick hesitated. "I'll invoke my right against self-incrimination."

"Wise move. How's your friend Raul holding up?"

Nick had paced his way to the kitchen and poured a cup of coffee. "He's hanging in there. Anything new on his drug case?"

"I spoke with your country prosecutor, Garcia. He said the police have someone in custody who admitted to planting the drugs, and he's dropping the charge."

"Good. Thanks for your help, and add your time to whatever you're charging me."

"Don't worry about that. How are you doing with all this turmoil?"

Nick took a sip. "Let's see. I've been accused of a crime I didn't commit, some fat cat is hounding me for it even though I proved my innocence, my friends are getting harassed, I got beat up, and I'm being vilified online. People are breaking into my house to plant evidence, and my girlfriend got punched in the face. All things considered, I'm having a swell time, Grand."

Grand laughed. "Keep your sense of humor, Nicholas. This will all be over soon."

"Does that appear likely, too?"

"Maybe a bit more definitive. I'll be in touch."

After he disconnected, Nick looked out the kitchen window at the deck. Felicia sat at the table, seeming to read a magazine. She angrily tossed the magazine aside and stared ahead. He recalled their earlier conversation.

Felicia's really been put through the wringer lately, and all because of me. She could've stayed out of my problem, but she didn't. She's stood beside me, no matter how much flak has come our way. She deserves something for all that pain and suffering.

He went to the den, found the phone number he needed in his address book, then placed an overseas call.

Late afternoon found Nick and Felicia at Cricket's, waiting for the evening crowd. The light rain of earlier had deposited small puddles on the deck that now reflected the bright sun.

Nick always thought of the almost-daily showers as a cleansing ritual, washing away the grime of the previous day like a hot shower after playing volleyball or gardening.

He stood near the inside bar, chatting with one of the servers, when his attention went to the front door. He felt his jaw tense when he spied Brannigan and Cortez walking in. *What the hell are they doing here?*

Nick strolled over and looked them up and down. "Unless you two are here for dinner, you made a wrong turn when you left Fort Lauderdale."

"We have a few questions," Cortez said.

"According to McCorkle, I'm off limits to you guys."

"We don't work for him."

Nick eyed him for a moment. "You realize that one phone call to my attorney gets you a harassment complaint, right?"

Cortez shrugged. "We'll take that chance. You gonna talk to us?"

"Like I have a choice?"

He escorted them to a corner table, away from the customers. They sat, and Nick maintained his wary gaze.

"What is it now?" he asked. "Are you here to tell me you uncovered new evidence that points to my guilt, or that I'm involved in some cover-up conspiracy? Perhaps you're still working on the theory that I offed Kristine Overman for my good buddy, Bianco."

"Nothing quite so dramatic," Brannigan said. "Are you acquainted with a drug dealer named Eddie Parks?"

Nick paused for a few moments. "I seem to recall that name. What about him?"

"How well do you know him?" Cortez asked.

"Passing acquaintance. We crossed paths on the Gold Flamingo."

"Did you know that the Overman girl was one of his customers, and she was getting her drugs from him?"

Nick's face broke into a grin as he laughed softly.

"You find this amusing?" Brannigan asked.

"You guys have your heads so far up your ass, it's pathetic. Kristine wasn't buying drugs from Parks. She was one of his suppliers."

The two detectives exchanged looks of involuntary surprise.

"How do you know that?" Cortez asked.

"Parks told me. I identified him from that security footage I showed you and I went to the boat to grill him about what happened the night of the murder."

"Did he happen to confess that he killed her?" Brannigan asked.

"No, but he told me about their business arrangement."

"Why didn't you say anything about this?"

Nick gave Brannigan a hard look. "I cleared myself, and handed you another suspect to look at. Do you expect me to do all of your work for you?"

Cortez leaned forward and pointed his finger at Nick. "You can skate around this all you want, but I still say you had a hand in her murder."

Nick looked at him for a few moments. "Tell me something, Detective. How much is J.P. Overman paying you to frame me?"

Cortez slowly began to stand but Brannigan placed his hand on his shoulder.

"Forget it, Ray. It's not worth it."

Cortez sat, radiating fury. "Accusing a cop of being on the take is a serious charge, Seven."

"So I've been told. So's murder."

"What do you know about Parks getting a beat-down on the Gold Flamingo a couple of nights ago?" Brannigan asked.

Nick's eyebrows went up a notch. "He did? I hadn't heard."

Brannigan nodded slowly. "Right. Like you hadn't heard

about Overman's drug habit until we told you."

Nick shrugged. "Sometimes you don't know people as well as you think you do. Anything else?"

The detectives stood.

"Not at the moment," Cortez said, "but we'll be in touch."

"Save yourself some grief and bring a subpoena with you next time," Nick said. "That is, if you can find a judge dumb enough to sign off on one."

He watched them leave but couldn't get his heart to stop racing. *Idiots. Between them and Overman hassling me, my life isn't worth shit at the moment. It's time to stop all this foolishness.*

Felicia sat down at his table. "What did those guys want this time?"

"More of the same. Apparently, they spoke with Parks, that drug dealer we busted. Rock's men must've given him his lumps. Of course they asked *me* about it."

Felicia shook her head. "Hon, we got to stop this nonsense. Those cops aren't gonna leave you alone, Overman's turnin' up the heat, and now Raul got dragged into it. Enough is enough."

Nick felt his brain start to function again. "You're right, it is."

"What're you gonna do?"

"You mean what are we gonna do."

"We, as in us, as in together?"

"Aren't you the one who said we're a team? We'll show those cops how it's done."

Felicia smiled. "Sounds good. Where do we start?"

"You said something the other night when we were having dinner on Rock's boat. You asked why his security people didn't catch the murder on the surveillance cams, and he said the only thing that gets their attention from outside is someone trying to sneak on board."

"What about it?"

"If his cameras are monitoring the water taxi and private

boat docks, that means they have video of everyone who came out that night."

Nick took out his cell phone and punched in Rock Bianco's private number. After a few rings he heard Rock's trademark growl of "Yeah?"

"It's Nick. I need a favor."

"Such as?"

"I need your tech guys to e-mail me the security footage from your landing decks the night of Overman's murder. I want to know everyone who came aboard the Gold Flamingo that evening. I'll need the security footage from your water taxi, too, but just for the hour immediately after the killing."

There was a brief pause. "I'll get 'em working on it. Those two dimwit cops were out here again."

"What did they want this time?"

"They were askin' about that pusher you busted."

Nick fought back laughter. "I hear he had a nasty accident."

"Yeah, I heard that, too. Poor bastard slipped and fell. They threatened me with an assault charge unless I helped them with their murder case."

"What help could you provide? You weren't involved."

"I think they're still tryin' to get me to implicate you."

Nick paused. "Send me that video footage. I'm bringing this to a halt."

Cain paced the hallway in the prisoner's wing of Founder's Hospital and looked at his watch. *What the hell's keeping Garcia? He said to meet him here at four and it's going on five.*

He looked up when he saw Garcia and a stenographer approaching.

"You're late," Cain said.

"Unavoidable. I spent the afternoon wrestling with one of J.P. Overman's lawyers."

"How did it go?"

Garcia chuckled. "Be glad you weren't there. That guy has nothing good to say about the way we do things down here."

"Did he buy our story about DeGarmo's paperwork getting lost?"

"Not before he threatened me with an order to show cause for why he can't see his client. I managed to put him off until tomorrow, so we need to get his statement now."

They went into the private room where DeGarmo was being guarded by a deputy. He was in bed, wearing a monitor that kept track of his vital signs, and his wrist was handcuffed to the bed rail. He scowled at Cain.

"What the hell kind of jail are you running here?" he demanded. "You grab me for some nuisance charge and the next thing I know, I'm wired for sound."

"Just looking after your health needs," Cain answered. "I spoke to the doctor and he suggests you lay off the booze and pay more attention to your diet."

DeGarmo smirked. "I noticed he's a Mexican. Probably got his diploma from one of those mail-order places in Costa Rica."

Garcia cleared his throat. "Mr. DeGarmo, I'm Manuel Garcia, the Monroe County Prosecutor. Sheriff Cain relayed your request to enter into a plea agreement for the charges pending against you. What do you have in mind?"

"Six months, with credit for time served," DeGarmo said.

"That's pretty light, considering," Garcia answered. "If I take this to trial, you could be looking at two years, minimum."

"For what?"

"Drug possession, breaking and entering, and simple assault."

"The amount of drugs falls under misdemeanor weight, I entered that guy's house by mistake, and I was defending myself against someone who attacked me."

"Maybe if you were in Miami, but you don't have any friends down here. What are you offering for my generosity?"

DeGarmo stared at him for a few moments. "You want the person who sent me here, and I can give him to you."

Garcia pulled up a chair while the stenographer set up her laptop. Cain leaned against the door jamb and crossed his arms over his chest.

"Before I take your statement," Garcia said, "have you been made aware of your rights?"

"Yeah, yeah," DeGarmo grumbled. "I got it."

"Are you still waiving your right to have an attorney present?"

He let out an irritated breath. "Yeah. Let's get on with it, Pedro."

"Fine. Why did you plant drugs in Raul Barba's car?"

"I was following orders. I was told to make the guy look like a dealer so he'd get arrested."

"Did you place the anonymous call to the Sheriff's office telling them that he had marijuana in his vehicle, and provide his license plate number?"

DeGarmo hesitated. "Yeah, I did that."

"Did you also break into the home of Nick Seven?"

"Yeah, I did that, too."

"For what purpose?"

DeGarmo looked at him. "I was told to leave something there that would make him look guilty in the murder of Kristine Overman."

"Your intention was not to steal anything from the home?"

"No."

"Who told you to do these things?"

DeGarmo looked at him for a few moments. "Our deal stands, right?"

"I'll live up to my end, provided your story checks out."

"I was following J.P. Overman's instructions."

"Overman himself specifically told you to plant drugs and do a home invasion?" Cain asked.

"He called me and asked me to do him a favor. He said he'd appreciate it very much, and he'd make it worth my time."

"How did you know that's what he meant by doing him a favor?"

DeGarmo looked at him. "I've been working for him for five years. That's how he talks when he wants something done. I do him a favor, and he does one for me, usually in my paycheck. He told me what he had in mind, and I did it."

"He pays you a bonus for these crimes?" Garcia asked.

"Yeah."

"What other favors have you done for Overman?"

DeGarmo was silent for a moment. "Let's just say this wasn't the first time he called on my special talents."

"Come on, DeGarmo," Cain challenged. "Give us a hint. If what you're saying is true, we need some way to verify these little favors you've been doing for money."

DeGarmo looked down for a moment. "Last year, when Overman was doing some buy-out of a company in Sarasota, the owner wasn't playing along. The Man called on me for a favor, as he put it."

"What did you do?"

DeGarmo looked at Cain. "If you check the police records, you might run across a car accident involving the gentleman in question. He was on his way home one night when his brakes failed. If you don't believe me, I'll show you my bank records. That little job was worth a hundred grand, deposited the day after the mark was involved in a three-car pile-up during rush hour."

Cain decided to play his hunch. "Did one of those favors you mentioned involve the death of Kristine Overman?"

DeGarmo shook his head. "No way you're pinning that one on me. I draw the line at murder."

"Nice to know you have scruples," Cain said. "Are you saying you had nothing to do with what happened to her on the Gold Flamingo?"

"Check my credit card receipts. The night that went down, I was at Tango's in South Beach with some friends." He paused. "And no, I don't know who might've killed her."

Garcia gave his stenographer instructions to type up the statement and get it signed and notarized. He and Cain stepped into the hall.

"What do you think?" Cain asked. "Will this hold up in court?"

"Follow up and get me some hard evidence. If you can verify what DeGarmo said about his prior acts, it might also play well in the court of public opinion."

Cain looked at him raised eyebrows. "Geez, Manny, you're actually loosening up a little. There may be hope for you yet."

"Don't get used to it. I just don't like the J.P. Overmans of the world thinking they can do whatever they damn well please and get away with it."

CHAPTER TWENTY-ONE

Binge-watching TV programs was a popular fad, thanks to fan-favorite shows that appealed to a certain mindset and age demographic. Nick had never understood the appeal, but was now experiencing it firsthand. Rock had forwarded the surveillance videos Nick requested, and he and Felicia had spent the past three hours watching it on the TV in the living room. They had settled into the couch to view a seemingly endless parade of gamblers coming and going from the Gold Flamingo.

Nick exhaled a deep breath. "I don't know how much more of this I can take."

"I'll bet you were a lotta fun on stakeouts."

"How are you not getting bored?"

"By distractin' myself with what people are wearin'. Have you noticed some of the outfits they have on?"

He chuckled. "Now that you mention it, those are some unique fashion statements. You can definitely tell the tourists from the locals. Whatever happened to dress casual?"

"It's been replaced by cargo shorts and ugly shirts."

Felicia took a handful of cashews from the bowl sitting between them. "What are you hopin' to find in all this?"

"Anyone who doesn't belong."

"How you gonna know if they don't belong? You think they'll have a big sign that says *killer* hangin' around their neck?"

Nick ignored her jab but clicked the index on the video feed to see what timeframe they were watching. They had fast forwarded through the two hours preceding the time of the killing, and no familiar faces had popped up yet. Nick stopped the action and selected the file that documented the water taxi's return trip to the mainland after the killing.

"What are you switchin' to?"

"Right after she went overboard. I want to see who left the boat."

They watched the action unfolding as people boarded the outbound water taxi. Nick's mind began to wander as he lost focus. *This will probably turn into another blind alley. I don't know any of Kristine's friends, and if it was a contract killing, I'd never be able to ID the killer. I think this was a waste of time.*

His mind suddenly snapped back into focus when he saw something. He used the remote to freeze the images on the screen, then stared for a few moments.

"What do you see?" Felicia asked.

"Parks, our friendly neighborhood pusher. He left the boat ten minutes after Kristine went overboard."

"Yeah, he told us that when we grilled him. What about it?"

Nick pointed at the screen. "Look who else decided to call it an early night. That looks like the guy we saw in the video, the one who strangled Kristine."

Felicia got up and stepped closer to the screen. "This only shows him from behind and a partial side view, but it could be the same guy. Same build, hairstyle, and clothes, but he kept his face away from the camera."

Nick stared at the image as something bubbled up from the inner recesses of his mind, something he had seen but had only registered as a subliminal blip. *My eyes saw it but my conscious mind didn't notice it before now. What are the odds?*

"You know all that stuff we got about Overman's mental breakdown, and the drugs Kristine had on her when she was killed?"

"Yeah."

Nick looked at her. "Bombs away."

Morning came early for Nick. After what he had discovered the evening before, he was anxious to put all the pieces in place and bring an end to this living nightmare. He had verified what he suspected, and was now ready for the showdown. Felicia had already posted on the chat board, and the responses were good. He placed a call to Bill Ceretta.

"Hey, it's Seven," he said when his call was answered. "You been following that chat board?"

Ceretta chuckled. "Yeah, great spin you put on that stuff. I hope you never get mad at me."

"How would you like to witness his latest meltdown?"

"What do you have in mind?"

"According to Overman's site, he's holding another press thing this afternoon. You going?"

"I thought it might be good for a laugh. Why?"

"Get me a couple of passes to get in and you'll see. Just do your homework before you go."

"I'll meet you there."

Nick hung up, then turned his attention to the computer screen, pulling up the casino video showing his encounter with Kristine. He went frame by frame until he found what he was looking for, then zoomed in on a figure standing in the background. He printed off the image and retrieved the close-up photos Felicia had printed from the killing. He used a magnifying glass to examine the killer's left hand, specifically the item that had caught his attention earlier. His gaze pivoted between two shots of Kristine during the killing, one before she was strangled and one immediately before she was flung overboard. He held up the photo of the pendant DeGarmo had dropped in their home and made comparisons. *The final piece. She had it on in the casino and when she went to the observation deck, but it wasn't there when she was thrown over.* He scrolled through some photos he had accessed in the local newspaper archives, then saved three of them.

Felicia came into the den carrying a cup of coffee. She leaned against the door frame with one leg cocked. Nick cast his gaze from head to toe, taking in her loose shirt, unbuttoned, with nothing underneath.

"Wow," he commented. "You really know how to dress up a room."

Felicia blew him a kiss. "Glad you don't get after me for feelin' at home."

"I've always respected your native customs."

She gestured at the photos on his desk. "You find what you were lookin' for?"

Nick looked at the array in front of him. "Yeah. I called Ceretta, and we're meeting at Overman's press conference this afternoon. Want to come along?"

She shrugged. "I guess. What do you hope to accomplish there? All he's gonna do is attack you and the press again."

"I'm going to call him out on all that stuff we've been posting. With any luck, he'll break down in front of the media he hates so much."

"Been thinkin' about that. For a guy who's such a narcissist, he acts like he hates the press, but he's always lookin' for ways to get in the papers or on TV."

"That backs up the profile you did. You pegged him as a sociopath with an unnatural need to be the center of attention. When he can't control the situation, he finds a way to manipulate the facts." Nick looked at the photos again. "Only this time, his shell game won't work."

Felicia's brow furrowed. "What shell game?"

"The one he devised to take the focus away from who really killed Kristine and place it on me."

She was silent for a few moments. "You know who did it, don't you?"

"I think so, but I need proof. I'm hoping to get it this afternoon."

Felicia sauntered over to a chair. Nick looked at her posture, sort of casual-but-lazy, her body resting comfortably with one leg thrown over the chair arm, giving him the full exposure. *Damn, I wish she wouldn't do that when I need to concentrate.*

"Angel, please don't take this the wrong way. I appreciate your body, and I respect your natural desire to walk around the house half-naked. In fact, I like it. But when you do that when I'm trying to focus on something, it's . . . uh . . . distracting."

Felicia gave a demure smile then held her coffee cup between her legs. "That better, tough guy?"

Nick cleared his throat. *Man, that's erotic as hell, like a Leroy Niemann painting come to life.* "It's getting there."

He grabbed his phone and placed a call to Ted Cain.

"This is Nick," he said when Ted answered. "How do things stand with your case against DeGarmo?"

"And a pleasant good morning to you, too. He copped to everything on the record, including setting up Raul and breaking into your home."

"Anything else?"

Ted paused for a moment. "He claims Overman ordered him to do what he did."

Nick felt his pulse kick up a notch. "How strong is your evidence?"

"Honestly, I'd feel better if we had more corroboration. DeGarmo isn't the most credible witness, given his police record."

"He must've given you something tangible."

"He says Overman pays him a bonus for these bits of larceny, and we were able to verify one job he pulled a few months ago. DeGarmo led us to the money trail, the one Overman used to pay him for services rendered."

Nick looked at the screen again. "Do you like to play long-shots when you go to the dog track, Ted?"

"Depends on their pedigree. Why are you asking?"

"I'm going to email you some photos. If you wouldn't mind, have someone show them to the crew on the taxi boat Bianco uses, and ask if this person was a passenger the night of the seventeenth, between nine-thirty and ten."

Ted chuckled. "What's the gag, Nick?"

"No gag. I'm giving you a chance to solve the Overman homicide. Might even get you elected president of the Florida Sheriff's Association."

"Are you saying you know who killed her?"

"I'm saying I have a strong hunch, but I don't have the authority to gather all the facts." He hesitated for a moment. "Is the statement you got from DeGarmo enough to bring Overman in for questioning?"

There was a long, uncomfortable silence.

"Nick, have you lost your mind? You actually expect me to bring in one of the most powerful men in the state based on the word of a former cop who makes Dirty Harry look like Mother Teresa?"

"If he were some regular Joe who ran a garage or a deli, you wouldn't think twice about it. What are you afraid of?"

"Gee, I don't know. Maybe that he could swat me like a fly with his legal dream team. Not all of us have the luxury of a government pension to live off of, you know. Some of us have to work for a living."

Nick exhaled. "Ted, I think I can get Overman to break down. He's holding a press briefing this afternoon at the Eden Roc in Miami Beach, and I'm going to be there."

"What's your game plan?"

"I'm going to challenge him on all this stuff that's been posted. If he follows his usual pattern, he'll get rattled and say something without thinking first. If you were there with a material witness warrant, it could be the stake to drive though his heart."

Ted was silent for a few moments. "What time is this press conference?"

Nick grinned. "Two o'clock. Will I see you there?"

"Let me see what I can do."

He disconnected, then looked at the photos again, reassuring himself of what he suspected.

"You really think you can get this guy to blow his cork?" Felicia asked.

"I'm gonna give it one helluva shot."

Chapter Twenty-two

The Eden Roc Hotel was situated on the sandy shore at the north end of Miami Beach, overlooking the bright blue Atlantic. The decades-old resort, once the winter destination for the wealthy snowbird set, had undergone a resurgence in popularity thanks to a new, younger crop of self-made moguls with a taste for nostalgia and luxurious pampering. The white stucco building was surrounded by tall palm trees that cast shadows over the property.

Nick and Felicia entered the marbled art deco lobby and located the banquet room where J.P. Overman would be holding court. Nick saw Ceretta pacing in the hall outside the room, checking his watch. He looked up as they approached.

"I was afraid you weren't going to show," he said.

"Traffic," Nick said. "Are you ready for this?"

He chuckled. "Oh, yeah. I boned up on that stuff from the chat board." He handed Nick two plastic-encased press passes. "Let's do it."

They entered the large room after a security guard waved a hand scanner over them. Ceretta guided them to a spot in the middle of the room. Nick looked at the crowd and estimated that there were twenty-five people in attendance. The TV reporters had brought camera operators, who focused on the small stage. Promptly at two, Overman entered from a door behind the podium, dressed in his usual suit and tie. He approached the podium and began.

"Good afternoon," he said. "I've called you all here today to provide an update on my request to the Attorney General to launch an independent investigation into my daughter Kristine's death. To date, my pleas for justice have gone unanswered. This official was elected by you good citizens, but he has refused to honor my request. I am appealing to every voter out there to contact not only the Attorney General, but your elected representatives. Let them know of your displeasure. This kind of negligence cannot be allowed to continue."

Nick listened as Overman rattled on for a few minutes, offering disparaging opinions about the AG and the county prosecutor. He also managed to make a few snide remarks about Nick while he was at it. Nick suppressed a laugh when Overman compared him to a Colombian drug lord. *This is gonna be so much fun.* When Overman said he would take questions, Nick stepped out from behind Ceretta and cupped his hand around his mouth.

"When did you stop beating your wife?" he called out.

Nick stepped behind Ceretta and crouched slightly to hide. Overman quickly swiveled his head from one side to the other, scanning the room.

"Who said that?" he demanded. "I didn't . . . I mean I never . . . How dare you ask me something like that. Ask relevant questions or I'll have you removed."

Nick leaned out again. "Is it true you were hospitalized in Tampa five years ago for mental illness?"

There was muted laughter and muttering throughout the room as the reporters attempted to hide their smiles.

"I don't know what kind of lies you people have been making up about me, but I will not dignify that with a response," Overman boomed. "Stick to the facts."

"What is your reaction to recent reports that your academic record was falsified?" a reporter asked.

Overman appeared to be getting flustered. "My academic record is none of your business. I graduated *magna cum laude* from a respected university, which is more than I can say about any of you parasites and leeches. The next question had better be on topic or this briefing is over."

Ceretta spoke up. "Can you comment on a report that you paid a member of your private security detail, a former Miami police officer, to commit several felonies on your orders?"

Felicia leaned close to Nick and whispered, "How did he hear about that?"

"I don't know, but it's good stuff," Nick whispered back.

Overman's face turned red and his breathing seemed labored. "I will not comment on that! I take no responsibility for what my employees do, and I will not be insulted by such a vulgar accusation. We're here to discuss the investigation into my daughter's murder, period. Is that clear?"

A woman reporter from one of the TV stations spoke up. "Mr. Overman, there have been recent reports that your son was involved in several violent assaults against women, and that you paid these victims not to press charges. It's also been reported that you paid for one of them to have an abortion. Your reaction?"

"I—I—I will not respond to that," he stammered. "This is nothing more than a witch hunt, a vendetta propagated by the phony news organizations to embarrass and discredit me. How can you call yourself a journalist, asking me an inappropriate question like that?" He turned to face one of his aids who was standing nearby. "I want the name of that reporter's employer, and she is to be banned from future press briefings. Is that clear?"

Low-key muttering among the reporters filled the room. Nick decided it was time to go for the jugular. "Is there any truth to the rumor that your daughter Kristine was selling drugs?" he called out.

Overman looked as though he was about to explode. His gaze narrowed and his jaw tightened even more when he looked in Nick's direction and made eye contact.

"That is a bold-faced lie, and you know it! You planted those drugs on her when you killed her, you scum!" He pointed his finger in Nick's direction. "That's the man who killed my daughter. He's the one you should be directing these inflammatory questions at. He alone is responsible."

"Who are you covering for, J.P.?" Nick chided.

Overman silently fumed for a few moments. His left eye began to twitch and his gaze took on more intensity. When he responded, it was in a lower voice, laced with anger. "We all know what this is really about. This is nothing more than a smear campaign, a way to make me look bad." He slowly wagged his finger. "This is the same way the SEC went after me when I tried to buy Continental Broadcasting a few years ago. They trotted out bullshit allegations and lies to make me look incompetent to their stockholders. It didn't work then, and it won't work this time."

"Are you refusing to answer the last question?" Ceretta asked. "Do you in fact know who killed your daughter, and are you shielding this person from the police?"

Overman slammed his fist on the podium. "Enough! I will not be subjected to this kind of muckraking sensationalism. You fools, with your phony questions and made-up theories, only want to harass me. That's the way it is with you people. You're all fake reporters, and you make up what you call *facts*. Do you write about the good things I've done for this state? Of course not. You're only interested in the kind of trash that sells your worthless publications and gets people to watch your phony news programs."

More chatter from the reporters filled the room. Nick's attention went to the right side of the dais, where he saw Ted Cain, accompanied by a uniformed officer and another man in a jacket and tie. Cain got the attention of one of Overman's aids, spoke with him, then showed him a document. The man read it and handed it back. He walked to the podium, placed his hand over the microphone and spoke with Overman. Overman looked at Cain for a moment then approached him. After a brief discussion, he was led out of the room.

The press immediately began shouting questions at Overman's people who were still present, asking what was going on. Nick heard questions in the vein of "Is he under arrest?" and "Why did the police take him away?"

Ceretta turned to Nick. "Not bad. You really rattled his cage."

"Is that the reaction you were hoping for?"

"Pretty damn close. What was up with Cain taking him out of here?"

Nick thought for a moment. "Call me later."

"Are you promising me an exclusive?"

Nick shrugged. "I'm not promising anything." He hesitated. "Those other reporters were quick to jump on the stuff we posted on that chat board. Do they really follow everything that closely?"

Ceretta glanced down and grinned. "It's possible they were tipped off by a mutual acquaintance who may have called some of his friends in the business."

Nick chuckled. "Tell your friend I said thank you."

He and Felicia left the room and headed for the parking lot.

"Congratulations for makin' him fall apart," she said.

"It's all about lighting the fuse and then knowing when to step away."

A couple of hours after the big meltdown, Nick parked in the lot outside Cain's office. He sat for a few moments, reflecting. *Every so often, people get the chance to face down and slay their personal demons. The showdown is like overcoming a deep-seated fear or phobia. Some are more traumatic than others. I don't scare easy, but still, I feel myself flinch at the last moment. It's almost like I doubt the outcome. And this is one of those times.*

He went inside. The desk sergeant directed him to an interrogation room down the hall. Nick approached the door, then paused to take a deep calming breath before going inside. His head throbbed slightly, signaling the start of another headache, but he ignored it. *In for a dime, in for a dollar.*

J.P. Overman sat at the table, his trademark scowl on prominent display. He was accompanied by J.P. Junior, who hadn't inherited his old man's fashion sense, opting for the beach bum look with a wrinkled tropical shirt and khakis, offset by a couple of days' worth of stubble and unkempt hair. Also present was an older man in a suit, whom Nick assumed was one of Overman's lawyers. Garcia sat off to the side. Ted Cain looked at Nick.

"Have a seat," he said. "This is Mr. Overman's attorney, Morris Bergstrom. I believe you know everyone else."

"What the hell is he doing here?" Overman demanded.

"Nick has a stake in this," Ted answered.

"I will not be in the same room with this hoodlum," Overman stated.

Nick sat. "Why don't you just shut up and listen for a change? Maybe you'll learn something."

Overman gave him a narrowed look that communicated more than a string of obscenities.

"Mr. Garcia, you have no case against my client," Bergstrom said. "Dragging him down here on a frivolous conspiracy charge? You're opening yourself up to a host of civil suits."

"The judge who authorized that warrant didn't think it was frivolous," Garcia said. "Neither did I when I applied for it."

Bergstrom leaned over the table. "Your so-called case is a pile of dust. You're basing your claim on the word of a broken-down cop who was let go for being a public menace. He's totally unreliable."

"He must not have been too unreliable, or your client wouldn't have hired him," Cain said.

Overman snorted. "That drunk is your best witness against me? You have a serious problem, Cain. I'm sure the voters will be interested in hearing about it come election time, along with whatever else I can dig up on you. If that doesn't take away that badge of yours, I have other methods."

Ted gave Overman an icy look. "Mr. Bergstrom, perhaps you'd like to remind your client about the penalty for threatening a police officer."

"Mr. Overman didn't mean anything out of line," Bergstrom said. "He's merely frustrated by this situation."

Ted glanced at Nick before continuing. "That's only one of the reasons we invited you here today. Nick, you're up."

Nick glanced at Overman and caught his killer stare. There was a challenge in Overman's demeanor, a how-dare-you-fuck-with-me look. Nick opened the envelope he had brought with him and took out some photos which he laid on the table.

"These were taken by the security cameras on the Gold Flamingo the night Kristine was killed," he said before passing one of them along. "This first one shows our confrontation in the casino. I want you to take note of the necklace she has on." He paused. "It's the same one your man DeGarmo tried to plant in my home the other night."

"That's fascinating, but what's your point?" Bergstrom asked.

"It wasn't on her body when she went overboard, and the police didn't find it at the murder scene. How did DeGarmo get it?"

"If DeGarmo had the young woman's jewelry in his possession, you should be talking to him," Bergstrom said. "It would be logical for him to have it if he killed her."

"DeGarmo has an alibi for the time of the murder," Ted said. "We verified it. Go on, Nick."

He passed along two other photos. "These are from the observation deck where Kristine was killed. As you can see, the killer was apparently left-handed, the way he automatically slapped her in what appeared to be a fit of rage. Take note of his left hand in the shot after he delivered the backhand slap. It took me a while to identify it, but the ring he's wearing looks like the Overman family crest. I remember Kristine telling me once that everyone in the family got a signet ring with that design." He paused. "Just like the ring you're wearing on your left hand, J.P."

Overman's scowl intensified, and he threw Garcia a nasty look.

"Are you just going to sit there and let him talk to me this way?"

Garcia shrugged. "I'm here as an observer. Sheriff Cain is conducting this interrogation, and he's doing a bang-up job."

Bergstrom slowly shook his head. "If this is all you have . . ."

"Actually, there's a bit more," Nick said, then looked at Junior. "By the way, it was nice running into you the other night, although I was a bit sore afterward."

"What're you talkin' about?" Junior said. "I haven't seen your sorry ass in years."

Nick slowly nodded. "I guess it was your twin who beat the shit out of me outside my club, huh?"

"My son has been at my home in Bal Harbour every night," J.P. stated.

"Right. You always covered your kids' asses, no matter how much trouble they got into. Some things never change."

Overman gave him another killer stare. "Seven, I don't know what game you're playing here, or what con you're running with your friend, the sheriff, but you're up against me now, in person."

"And loving every minute of it," Nick retorted, then

addressed Bergstrom. "In reference to your earlier point about Kristine's necklace, the only way DeGarmo could've gotten it is if your client gave it to him." He hesitated. "And the only person he could've gotten it from is the killer. That would be you, Junior."

Junior's eyes widened in surprise. "What? You're crazy. I wasn't even there."

Nick passed along another photo. "This shows you in the casino when Kristine and I had our confrontation. I didn't notice you right off, because you were standing in the background." He showed two more. "These are from the water taxi Rock Bianco uses, and they were taken shortly after Kristine was thrown overboard. I couldn't help noticing that one of the passengers bears an amazing resemblance to you, Junior."

J.P. looked at the photos then slammed them onto the table. "You're full of shit. These images don't prove anything, and they could have been taken at any other time."

"I don't think so," Ted interrupted. "When Nick brought this to my attention, we showed your son's DMV photo to the crew working that night. Three of them positively identified him as being a passenger."

"By the way," Nick said, "where's your ring, Junior? Do you only wear it for special occasions, like beating your sister to death?"

An awkward silence shrouded the room. Overman looked intently at his son, his jaw tightening and his complexion getting flushed. Junior's gaze examined the table.

"You stupid mental midget," Overman said. "If you weren't such a stunningly incompetent moron, we wouldn't be in this mess. You never could do anything right."

Junior raised his head and gave Overman a fiery look. "I'm stupid? Look how you fucked everything up. Keep your mouth shut and let me handle it, you said. You've handled it, all right. What do we do now, daddy dearest? You gonna buy my way out of this one, too?"

Overman's face flushed red with anger. "If you'd use your brain once in a while, I wouldn't have to do anything. I'm always bailing you out of one screw-up after another. Why can't you man up and stop being a major disappointment?"

Nick held up his open palm. "Save that for Dr. Phil. Why did you do it, Junior?"

Junior was silent for a few moments. When he responded, it was in a low subdued tone, almost a mumble.

"I didn't mean to kill her. I went out there to talk to her, to tell her to stop messing with drugs. We argued and she hit me." He slowly wagged his head. "I told her to stop, but she just kept hitting me and calling me names. She knew how much I hated that, but she wouldn't stop. I just . . . lost it."

He raised his head and nervously shifted his gaze from one person to another around the table. "It wasn't my fault. Don't you people get that? I told her to stop hitting me but she wouldn't. I just wanted to talk to her, to get her to stop messing with the drugs, but she just laughed at me. Then she started hitting me." He stopped and cast his gaze down again. "It wasn't my fault."

"Why did you care if she was doing drugs?" Nick asked.

After a momentary pause, Overman senior spoke up.

"Kristine's habit had gotten out of control. I tried getting her into a rehab program, but she refused. It was bad enough she was using that poison, but I found out she was selling. It was only a matter of time before it became public, and it would have ruined everything."

Nick's brow furrowed in confusion. "Let me see if I understand this. You were worried about tarnishing your good name, so you sent your son out there to kill your youngest daughter?"

Overman gave him a hard, penetrating stare. "Of course

not. I told him to stop her, to make sure she wasn't involved in that business." He hesitated. "When he told me what happened, I ordered him to keep quiet about it."

Nick nodded. "When you found out I was there and that Kristine and I had argued, you thought you had the perfect scapegoat to take the focus off Junior. Not a bad plan."

"You heard him. Kristine teased and mocked him and he lost control. It was an unavoidable accident."

"Your kids are never responsible for their actions, are they?" Nick said. "Kristine gets picked up for DUI, and you bribe the cops to make it go away. Junior slaps his women around, and you buy their silence. He kills Kristine during a temper tantrum, and you try to frame me for it. You're one sick son of a bitch, J.P."

Overman gave him a defiant look. "I've worked my whole life to give this family what it's entitled to. Kristine was no different. I don't know why she chose to become a drug dealer, a common street hustler. There was no reason for it. She had everything she ever could have wanted."

"Except her own identity," Nick said.

Overman pointed his finger and looked as though he was about to respond, but he abruptly stopped, lowered this hand and cast his gaze down.

"Mr. Garcia," Bergstrom said, "you can't charge young Overman here with the murder, since you have no jurisdiction."

"You're right, I can't," Garcia agreed. "But the Broward County prosecutor can, and I'm sending him the file, along with the video of this meeting. As to those other charges against Mr. Overman, Senior, I'm moving forward."

"I'm sure we can work something out," Overman said. "Both you and Cain are up for re-election. I have an excellent campaign team I can place at your disposal, along with some donors who owe me favors."

Garcia shook his head. "Your money's no good here."

Garcia and Bergstrom continued bantering while Nick sat back and stared at Overman. His sullen gaze was cast downward. He remained silent. He actually appeared rather pathetic. *If this is what wealth does to you, I'll keep working for a living.*

Cain called for a stenographer to take their statements. Nick marveled at both men's interpretation and embellishment of the facts. *Around and around it goes, one more spin cycle with the truth. Let's see his press corps get him out of this one.*

Nick suddenly felt claustrophobic and left the room. He leaned against the wall, took a few deep calming breaths, and noticed something. *When I went in there, I thought I was getting another headache, but now I feel better.*

Cain joined him. "You okay?"

Nick took a moment before responding. "I'm good."

"I know this was tough for you to do, but thanks."

"For what?"

"Sticking with it and seeing that the right thing was done. Is there anything you need from me?"

Nick looked at him. "Yeah. Send a copy of Overman's statement to my buddies, Brannigan and Cortez. Maybe they'll leave me alone."

Cain chuckled, resting his hand on Nick's shoulder. "You got it."

CHAPTER TWENTY-THREE

Three days had passed since the big showdown, and life seemed to be getting back to normal. Cricket's business had picked up, tourists packed the resorts, charter fishing boats were booked to capacity, and people sailed blithely through their days as though nothing had happened.

Nick sat in his office, his feet resting on the edge of the desk and a copy of the Miami newspaper in his hands. He read the latest coverage of the Overman downfall between sips of coffee. After skimming through the story, he folded the paper then tossed it into the trash can. *The son of a bitch will probably get a reality TV show out of this.*

He leaned his head back and closed his eyes. The events of the previous week came flooding back like a dam that had sprung a leak. *Can't help thinking how fate and circumstance always seem to get in the way. If we hadn't gone to the boat on that particular night, I wouldn't have run into Kristine, we wouldn't have argued in public, and she might not have been killed. Then again, with what she was involved in, it probably would have happened eventually. Karma can be a bitch.*

The pundits had all weighed in on J.P. Overman's fate, with some speculating that The Great Man had finally committed one public gaffe too many. His legal team was in talks with the Broward County prosecutor to make some kind of deal for Junior, and Overman's press people were working overtime to repair the damage to his reputation. Nick hadn't forgotten the harassment he had suffered from the Fort Lauderdale police, and wondered if Brannigan and Cortez had been reassigned to something less mentally strenuous, like parking meter enforcement.

Felicia entered the office carrying a cellophane-wrapped gift basket that was nearly half as tall as she was. She set it on the desk.

"What's this?" Nick asked.

"It just came."

They examined the basket filled with two bottles of French wine, imported cheeses, smoked salmon, fresh fruit, and a pair of red dice. Nick pulled off the card that was attached and read it aloud.

"Nick, thanks for your help. I always said you were the best. Don't be a stranger. Rock Bianco. P.S. — Enjoy the dice. They always come up seven."

Nick took out the dice and rolled them across the desk a couple of times. Each time, one revealed a five and the other showed a two. He laughed.

"He still knows how to rig the odds."

"That was nice of him to send this to you," Felicia said.

"He can be classy when he needs to be." Nick reached under the desk and retrieved a package that had arrived earlier. He handed it to Felicia.

"For me?" she asked.

"It has your name on it."

She tore off the brown paper and opened the box. She gasped when she took out a lead crystal footed dish.

"This belonged to my grandma," she said.

Nick watched her as she read the note the box contained. Felicia looked at him with a soft smile. He saw tears forming in the corners of her eyes.

"Why did my mom send this to me?"

"I called her and told her what happened during the break-in. When she heard how upset you were, she wanted you to have that." He paused. "She also said accidents happen, and she isn't mad at you. You really should call her."

Felicia set the dish on the desk then sat on Nick's lap. She gave him a lingering kiss.

"I'll do that," she said. "You're full of surprises."

He played with a strand of her hair. "I'm just looking out for you."

"I appreciate it." She placed her hand on the back of his neck. "I couldn't help noticin' how quiet you've been the past coupla days. I thought after this mess got settled, you'd get back to bein' yourself."

"I've been working on that."

"But?"

"I need to work harder."

"When you got me talkin' about my grandma, it made me remember somethin' she told me. *Felicia,* she'd say, *don't look for the rainbow before it rains.*"

Nick's brow furrowed. "That's nice, but what does it have to do with this?"

Felicia giggled and shrugged. "Prob'ly nothin', but it's the best I could come up with."

"I remember one my dad used to say — *Don't spend it before you got it.*"

"Was that the best advice anyone ever gave you?"

"No, I think the best was *Never date a girl with a gun.* I had a problem with that one."

Felicia lightly dragged her fingers across his cheek. "I remember."

"I remember a proposition I made to you about taking a trip home so you could visit your family."

"After everything that happened on our last trip, can't we just stay here?"

He peered into her soft eyes. "As you wish, angel."

You May Also Enjoy the Following from eXtasy Books Inc:

Cuban Fire
Tim Smith

Excerpt

Key West at two in the afternoon in late July had to be one of the hottest places on the planet. The thermometer topped out at 98 and the humidity easily added another 10 degrees. Even the faint but steady breeze that blew in from the Gulf did little to ease the discomfort and only served to make the palm fronds sway gently overhead.

Brad Swanson sipped his second Mojito of the afternoon while sitting waist-deep at the in-pool tiki bar of his hotel, wearing swimming trunks and no shirt. The water cooled off his lower parts, but his lean upper body was covered in a sheen of sweat. A middle-aged couple occupied stools on the other end of the oval bar, but the ones next to him were empty. He sipped his drink, then looked at the plastic cup. Not the best Mojito I've ever had, but not the worst either. That prize would go to a seafood restaurant with a phony tropical motif back home in Dayton, Ohio.

He set his cup on the bar, then looked around. About a dozen people spanning ages twenty to sixty were lazily swimming about, with another dozen stretched out poolside on chaises, absorbing as much Florida sun as they could stand. Occasionally one would dive into the water to cool off.

Brad glanced down at his torso and legs. His white skin had picked up some sun since his arrival, but at this point he looked more pink than tanned. He brushed his thick brown hair back from his face and noticed that it, too, dripped with sweat.

He had been in town for two days on an assignment for the newspaper he worked for in Ohio, writing a story on the latest hurricane that had ravaged the Keys a week earlier. The publication was a left-leaning tabloid that took great delight in pushing political buttons. His editor, a potbelly with no fashion sense, who belched too much, had sent him there to document what type of disaster relief the federal government wasn't providing for those who had lost their homes and livelihoods. Brad tried to recall the name of the last big blow — Rita, Thelma, Zelda? Something like that. It had been a long storm season and the weather folks had already exhausted this year's alphabet.

His problem wasn't with the assignment or taking a paid vacation in this tropical paradise, although he would've preferred it in December. His dilemma was that after spending two days traveling the lower and middle Keys, taking photos and interviewing impacted residents, his result was little more than a bunch of profanity-laced opinions he couldn't print. This is what I get for abandoning the novel festering in my soul and selling out to some radical rag, run by a publisher who's probably a closet communist. The bad thing is, when I get home in a few days, Potbelly is expecting to see an award-worthy exposé, but I haven't gotten squat so far. Maybe I'm too focused on it. I think I should spend the rest of the afternoon in this pool, at this bar, drinking too many of these so-so Mojitos.

Writer's block and a lack of creativity were only part of Brad's problem. He had made the trip alone because he recently broke up with his longtime girlfriend after he discovered she had been seeing a former boyfriend behind his back. The wound was still too fresh to dwell on and he thought this would take his mind off it. He'd been here many times and had hopes of meeting an attractive, unattached woman who was as lonely in paradise as he was. So far, he hadn't been that lucky.

I thought I had a shot with that woman I met at the raw bar last night, even though she was traveling with two of her friends. We seemed to hit it off and after a couple of drinks, I was ready to make my move when one of her besties said they decided to hit another bar. I forgot that even in paradise, when there are two or more women in a group, they hang out the do-not-disturb sign. Good thing my room has adult pay-per-view and hand lotion.

He took another sip, then nearly choked when he felt a splash of water from behind. He turned around in time to see a young woman climb onto the stool next to his. Brad automatically glanced over her frame, clad in a string bikini with a floral print. She looked to be about five-two and slender, with skin the color of café au lait and sun-bleached blonde hair with light brown streaks, cut into a shag style that covered her ears. Her figure was so petite that handle-with-care was the first thing that came to mind, while a posture that said don't-mess-with-me was the second.

She looked at him and offered a shy smile. "Sorry," she said in a thick Spanish accent. "Didn't mean to get you wet."

Brad recovered from his initial shock and smiled. "No problem. I was getting too hot anyway. It actually felt good."

The young woman giggled, making a pleasant sound, not nasal or forced. "You mind if I sit here?"

"Not at all." He hesitated for a moment to summon his courage. "Would you care for a drink?"

She released a deep breath. "Yeah, that'd be nice. Whatever you're havin'."

Brad signaled for the bartender and ordered her drink plus

a refill for himself. When they arrived, she took a long sip.

"Gracias," she said. "You not from 'round here, are you?"

"How can you tell?"

She gestured at his torso. "Not enough tan."

He laughed. "Looks like you got me. I'm from up north."

Her eyebrows arched. "Atlanta?"

"Further north than that. I'm from Ohio."

Her face scrunched in confusion. "Not sure where that is."

Brad eyed her for a moment. "I'm guessing you're not from around here either."

She shook her head. "Havana. Came here few years ago. What you do in this Ohio place?"

"Whatever it takes to survive. What do you do here?"

"Waitress at the Palm Garden. You ever been there?"

"No. Is it any good?"

She shrugged. "Not bad. Tourists sure like it, 'specially the ones who come from the cruise ships. What's your name?"

"Brad. What's yours?"

"Chiquita, like the banana."

He looked her over again. *I'd like to see what she could do with a banana.* "Pretty name. Are you staying here?"

She shook her head again. "I live in Olde Towne. This is my day off."

"I thought the pool was just for hotel guests."

She leaned in close and lowered her voice. "Supposed to be, but the bartender's a friend. He looks the other way when I sneak in. You not gonna bust me, are you?"

Brad laughed. "What fun would that be?"

She laughed with him. "I can think of things that would be whole lot more fun."

Makes two of us.

ABOUT THE AUTHOR

Tim Smith is an award-winning, bestselling author of romantic mystery/thrillers and contemporary erotic romance. He is also a freelance writer, editor, blogger, and photographer. His novels featuring former CIA agent Nick Seven have garnered several awards and international critical praise.